A Power of Old

A Shade of Vampire, Book 38

Bella Forrest

Also by Bella Forrest:

A SHADE OF DRAGON:

A Shade of Dragon 1
A Shade of Dragon 2
A Shade of Dragon 3

BEAUTIFUL MONSTER DUOLOGY:

Beautiful Monster 1
Beautiful Monster 2

A SHADE OF KIEV TRILOGY:

A Shade of Kiev 1
A Shade of Kiev 2
A Shade of Kiev 3

DETECTIVE ERIN BOND

(Adult mystery/thriller)

Lights, Camera, GONE
Write, Edit, KILL

For an updated list of Bella's books, please visit her website:
www.bellaforrest.net

Join Bella's VIP email list and she'll personally send you an email reminder as soon as her next book is out! Visit here to sign up:
www.forrestbooks.com

Contents

THE "NEW GENERATION" NAMES LIST

- **Arwen:** (daughter of Corrine and Ibrahim - witch)
- **Benedict:** (son of Rose and Caleb - human)
- **Brock:** (son of Kiev and Mona – half warlock)
- **Grace:** (daughter of Ben and River – half fae and half human)
- **Hazel:** (daughter of Rose and Caleb – human)
- **Heath:** (son of Jeriad and Sylvia – half dragon and half human)
- **Ruby:** (daughter of Claudia and Yuri – human)
- **Victoria:** (daughter of Vivienne and Xavier – human)

RUBY

I was so glad that we were back in Hellswan castle. I might have hated the gray, oppressive stone walls, and the constant lurking of muttering and secretive ministers, and even the fact that the sky was always the same gray as the stone, but it was what I'd reluctantly come to regard as 'home' in Nevertide. I felt almost safe here—safer than I did in Queen Trina's kingdom at least.

Yelena and Jenney had been clearing up after the kids, who had all fallen asleep in random spots in the living room—some lying on sofas, others on the carpet with only a cushion, the luckier ones were lying three or four to a bed.

Benedict's and Julian's beds were the only ones that remained empty. I suspected the rest of the kids avoided sleeping in them out of respect...but it might have been fear – as if their bad luck was contagious somehow.

It was dark outside. I should have been getting some rest but sleep just wouldn't come. We still had a bit of time before Benedict was expected to come stone-hunting. I dreaded seeing him under the control of the entity. I had heard what had happened to Yelena, and putting two and two together, I figured that Benedict had drained me too on the night before the disk trial. I didn't mention it to anyone—what would be the point? It just made my blood run cold to know that Benedict was capable of such destruction and power.

Ash came in through the servant's entrance and slammed the door shut behind him.

"Are you okay?" I asked, noticing the scowl and tense shoulders. Jenney gave him a wide berth.

"Just been to see if I can get my job back," he muttered.

I looked at Jenney. Apparently, it wasn't good news.

"Why?" I asked, my question genuine. After the trials, Ash hadn't expected to return to kitchen service.

"I don't really have much choice. The ministers here

definitely won't hire me now, since I've worked for Trina, and it's not like I can go back there again." He shrugged. "Maybe something will come up—but for now, it's best that I stay in the castle."

I hadn't thought about what might happen to Ash if he set Julian and I free from Queen Trina's dungeons. I thought the only reason he was staying in Hellswan was to protect me and Jenney.

"Ash, I'm so sorry—I didn't think—"

"It's fine—really. None of this is your fault, Shortie. Trust me when I say I'm happy not to be employed by a psychopath."

"I'm glad to have you back, Ash," Jenney chimed in. "It won't be like this forever."

"I know." He smiled, looking at me with warm eyes.

My stomach fluttered a bit, giving me goosebumps. It looked like Ash and I might be back on for the whole return-to-Earth plan, which suited me just fine. Repressing the thrill that ran through me at the thought of Ash arriving in The Shade, I smiled back.

Don't get ahead of yourself. It wasn't like we were any closer to getting out of here. And I hadn't even told Ash about The Shade or GASP.

"Well, it would be nice if the food around here improved," I teased.

"Don't push your luck, Shor—" Ash broke off, jerking his head in confusion.

What?

I meant to say the words as I thought them, but no sound came out. I tried again. Nothing.

What's going on?

Jenney and Ash simultaneously tried to talk. It would have been funny, if it wasn't for the freaky circumstances. I sighed, realizing what it was. I marched over to an old desk and pulled out a sheet of dusty parchment. Grabbing a piece of lead, I started to scrawl on the page:

'The pestilence of silence. I think it's one of the weird apocalyptic signs.'

I showed it to Ash and Jenney, and their shoulders sank. Yeah. This *really* wasn't ideal. Ash scratched his head, back to being irritated.

Then a thought occurred to me. This was supposed to be the *last* sign. We'd had the red rains and the fire of ice that had been promised in the books that Hazel and Tejus had found. What did reaching the last sign mean? Was the entity at full strength?

'The final one!' I scribbled down on the page, showing it to Ash. He nodded grimly. *Oh.* He'd already worked that out.

Guards burst through the door, and the sudden noise made us all jump. They looked at us, confused and bewildered. I shrugged at them. There was nothing any of us could do—we'd just have to wait this one out like all the others.

One of the guards stepped forward, holding out his hand in a 'stop' sign. He gestured to the rest of his men, pointing at the door.

I guess we stay here then.

I looked at Ash and he nodded, glancing toward the servants' entrance, undetected by the guards.

Right. If we needed to leave, we could go that way.

The guards retreated, and shut the door behind them. Just as that door shut, another opened, and Julian stumbled out looking bleary-eyed. Knowing that I wouldn't be able to go into any detail—and my mime skills weren't the best—I added another scribble to my paper and showed it to him.

'The pestilence of silence. I think it's one of the weird apocalyptic signs.

'The final one!

'Long story!'

Julian reached for his glasses, and then read what I'd written. He looked at me in bewilderment, going through the same motions of trying to speak that we'd all tried a moment ago. I waited till he had finished, patiently showing him the sign again. This time he just sighed with resignation. Yelena was next, coming up from the servants' quarters. When I tried to show her the paper she flapped her arm at me. 'Yeah, yeah,' her expression seemed to say, 'I got it."

I hid a smile. That girl was quite extraordinary for a human.

Scribbling again on the paper, I conveyed to the group that we should really go and find Hazel and Tejus—they might have an idea of what this meant in terms of the entity's rise to full power.

The others nodded, and Yelena started for the door, but I pulled her back, pointing to the servants' entrance.

We all headed down the narrow steps, and then through a deserted kitchen—some of the stoves had been left on, with great vats of unappetizing-looking stew still boiling. Ash went around dousing the fires with water, and then we made our way back up into the main body of the castle. From what I could see, it looked like all the servants had fled, but the ministers were still rushing around, panicking and wild-eyed. I repressed a smile. They must really be feeling the pain of not being able to mutter to one another.

An imposing male figure was marching along the hallway, ministers moving out of his way as he approached. When he came closer, I recognized the granite face of Memenion. I waved, and he nodded in greeting. As he approached us he peered curiously at Ash, but then turned to me and fished something from his pocket.

It was a letter, creased and stained with a faint splatter of dried red liquid. It was addressed to me in scrawled ink. I turned it over, and the signature of the Hellswan house was stamped on the back—below that were initials. 'Cdr. V.R'.

Commander Varga?

I looked up at Memenion and he smiled at me sadly. It *was* him, then. I could feel Ash giving me a puzzled look, and, not wanting to delay getting to Hazel and Tejus, I shoved it in the pocket of my robe.

I'll read it later.

Not knowing how to thank Memenion, I briefly placed

my hand on his arm in appreciation. He looked surprised, jerking it back, so I smiled awkwardly instead. I recalled the king's wife saying that they weren't closed-minded about humans, and I had believed her—though I couldn't help but wonder if our kind took some getting used to, just the way theirs did to us.

We continued our journey, watching more ministers sweep past us in frenzied panic. I didn't know where they were hurrying to or from—what did they think they could do?

When we got to the stairwell of Tejus's tower, there was no one around. I briefly wondered where all the guards had gone, but perhaps Tejus had sent them elsewhere…Didn't he feel that he and Hazel needed protection?

As we walked along the corridor to Tejus's living room, our path was suddenly blocked without warning. I realized what he had done. There were protective barriers up, blocking the entrance to his room. I sighed, further irked to see a conceited-looking lynx yawning at us obnoxiously before sticking his head up in the air and marching off.

I looked over at Ash in frustration.

What now?

He shook his head at the obvious, but unspoken

question. There was nothing to do but wait – it wasn't like we could call out to them or anything, we'd just have to stay put until they emerged. I hoped it wouldn't be long.

Yelena and Julian slumped against the walls, folding their arms and looking irritated. Eventually I joined them, not knowing what else to do. Ash paced up and down, intermittently scowling at the smug-looking lynx.

I must have dozed off for a while, because the next moment Ash was shaking me gently by the shoulders. I smiled at him sleepily, still only half-awake. He gestured back at the corridor – the cat was long gone. I jumped up, testing the air where the barriers had been. They were gone.

We quickly woke Julian and Yelena, and hurried toward our destination. Without knocking, we pushed open the heavy wooden doors and strode purposefully into Tejus's living room.

The first thing I saw was Tejus, standing by the window with a shaken expression on his face. He barely bothered to glance in our direction, looking off into the corner of the room instead. I followed his gaze, registering Hazel curled up in a ball, her face turned in my direction, but unseeing, as if I wasn't even there. She was wrapped up in a bed sheet, and her usually pale face was even whiter than normal. Her eyes were glazed, and I belatedly realized I was registering the tell-tale signs of extreme shock.

What the heck happened here?

HAZEL

I registered my friends entering through a haze of fear, hunger and bewilderment.

I didn't know how long it had been since my transformation had started to take effect. I could hardly look at Tejus without being infused with a crazy sensation of hunger. I wanted to gorge myself on his energy. It seemed so bright, so vibrant. It was like the gold threads of our past mind melds were constantly flowing through his body—through every single vein, every vessel.

How could I not want him?

How could I not want all of him?

All I seemed to be able to do was sit in the corner of the room, forcing my limbs to become like concrete, not allowing myself to move a single muscle in case my body launched itself toward Tejus and my mind took over, sucking his energy dry. Was this what it was like for him? Or was it because I was new to the sensation? It must be the latter, otherwise every single sentry in Nevertide would be locked in their homes, shaking and cursing themselves for wanting to do their loved ones harm.

Now I needed the rest of them gone.

Ruby's mind beckoned to me; she stood stone-still in the middle of the room, staring at me in confusion and deep, deep concern. Her mind was so strong though—I could practically feel it from where I sat.

Don't go there, Hazel—don't—you'll never forgive yourself.

I repeated my mantra and gritted my teeth, trying my best to keep my mind to myself and not try to go exploring others.

Not knowing what to do, I just sat there, hoping Tejus would warn Ruby away before she got too close. How could I be around anyone? I was a danger to them all— sentry or human, it didn't seem to make a difference.

How had my night with Tejus—the most amazing experience of my life—turned into such a nightmare?

Ruby took a step closer, arms rising to embrace me. I looked over at Tejus, my eyes imploring.

Help me! Stop her!

I drew my body closer inward, though it didn't seem to help—my mind had started to drift toward hers.

No!

Tejus strode forward and put out an arm to halt Ruby. She glared up at him furiously, trying to bat his arm away, but it was immovable. Ash took a step forward, placing a hand on Tejus's shoulder as a warning. I could tell that things were going to escalate quickly, but Tejus didn't respond with rage or aggression. He moved to stand in front of me, blocking my friends' view, with his arms held out to pacify them.

His eyes must have conveyed that he meant me no harm, because eventually they backed off. Ruby still looked mistrustful, but she stepped away with the rest.

A moment later, we were all distracted.

The door to the tower had started to rattle. It was soft at first, like a single gust of wind had shot down from the turret, and the door struggled to break free from its hinge. The rattling increased, the door slamming back and forth—it felt like there was someone on the other side, pushing and pulling against it. I half suspected the entire thing to fly from the frame, but instead, in the next moment, it went silent.

Next, a faint scratching sound came from behind the door. I looked at Tejus, my heart in my throat. It was a sound that would haunt my dreams for the rest of my life, the same sound I'd heard the night Benedict had tried to get into our living quarters.

Tejus nodded slightly, acknowledging the fact that we would not open the door—the creature behind it wasn't my brother. Not even close. I knew that, and Tejus knew that—but Julian, not seeing my warning glance at Tejus, and not knowing the hell we'd been through with Benedict, was obviously curious.

Moving surprisingly swiftly considering his weak state, he launched toward the door. He pulled at the handle, swinging it wide open before Tejus could stop him.

An impossibly strong wind hurtled into the room and sent books and cushions flying about the place, battering themselves against the walls and ceiling.

I watched, half rising to my feet, as my brother stepped into the room.

RUBY

I moved closer to Ash, and he reached down to clasp my hand. Beyond that, I was petrified. My first instinct on seeing Benedict was to run over and hug him. It had been swiftly replaced by a kind of grotesque horror—the twist of the malevolent smile and the glaze across his eyes sent shivers running through my body. Whatever that *thing* was, it wasn't Benedict. It might have looked like him in every way, but there was an unnatural and animalistic slyness about him that was far removed from the Benedict I knew and loved.

The furniture was flying about, and I ducked my head

as a huge book came flying toward me. I grabbed Yelena with my spare hand, making sure that the girl was standing out of harm's way. I didn't even think she felt me move her—she was fixated on Benedict, her body as pliant as a ragdoll's. Julian had been thrown back into the other corner of the room when the door burst open, and he stood, staring at his friend.

We watched, open-mouthed, as Benedict slowly raised his hand toward the wall on the far side of the room. The gray stones—centuries old—started to shift and rattle in the mortar. Dust started to cascade down the wall, then got swept up and blown in our faces. I shielded my eyes as they started to water, and through the blur of tears, I saw Tejus collapse—hitting the floor hard, with a heavy thump. Hazel jerked, almost as if his hurt was hers, but didn't move from her corner of the room.

Clearly Benedict had been syphoning off him, and apparently found him unsatisfactory. I held my breath, knowing that one of us would be next.

Yelena opened her mouth in a silent scream.

At the same time, the stones in the wall blew apart, sending shards ricocheting off the walls and skidding across the floor. A large piece catapulted toward Hazel, who bent double in pain as it slammed into her.

I looked back at the wall, and once the debris and dust cleared, small, bright stones of different tones and hues flickered in a pattern like Christmas tree lights. I didn't know if it was my imagination or not, but the stones looked as if they were humming and moving of their own accord—like they were *alive*.

Ash pulled me backward, moving us aside as Benedict started to walk across the room. Yelena was panting heavily now, her body growing limp as if it were an effort to stand. I let go of Ash's hand and held her to me, trying to keep her upright. The malevolent smile was still plastered across Benedict's face. Suddenly I felt unaccountably angry, and it took away the fear that had been pounding through me ever since I'd laid eyes on Hazel. I wanted to wipe that smug smile off Benedict—or the entity's—face.

How DARE you!

I was sick of fending off disasters, constantly under attack, from one evil of Nevertide to the next. I jerked forward, forgetting myself and the fact that I was next to useless against the power of the entity. Ash grabbed hold of me around the waist, tightening his grip.

I watched, frustratingly helpless, as Benedict reached up

and took one of the bright stones from the wall. When he touched it, it shone brighter than the rest—a sickly yellow light that bathed us all in its glow. With perfectly measured and relaxed movements, Benedict pocketed the stone in his robe. Turning, he walked back across the room and disappeared through the doorway. I heard the clunking of his footsteps on the stone staircase that led to the tower, and then nothing.

Julian slammed the door shut. Yelena's body gave way, and Ash caught her before she fell to the floor. He carried her over to the sofa and placed her on it. Tejus started to rise as well, using the wall beside him to balance.

How did he even get here—by bird?

Not able to wait another moment, I pulled the door open and hurtled up the steps to the tower.

Breathless, I reached the top in record time, but as I looked around I saw nothing, not even a tell-tale shadow in the sky that would indicate he'd escaped with a vulture. It was as if he'd completely disappeared into thin air.

Is that even possible?

Under the control of this mysterious entity, maybe anything was possible.

The wind had died completely, and the night was silent.

I was about to turn around and go back inside when I heard the scatter of small stones coming from below me on the tower.

I leaned over the balustrade, and looked down. In the moonlight, I could just make out a dark figure, scuttling down the wall as if it was no effort at all. I leaned a little further out, disbelieving. Suddenly it stopped, looking up at me, Benedict's face pale in the moonlight, with a smug, evil smile, staring right back at me.

After a pause, he continued his journey. As I turned away from the side of the tower, I couldn't help but think Benedict had just lost any part of him that was still human.

ROSE

An hour later, our joy at finding the portal was becoming short-lived. Corrine and the other witches were doing all that they could, but the thick, tar-like substance wasn't budging. Corrine was getting tired, her face gradually losing its color as she did everything within her power to force it open.

The sea was becoming choppier as the sun started to set. The waves were leaping up and smacking against the floats of the sea plane and soaking the interior. I could taste sea salt in my mouth, making me thirsty. Caleb clutched my hand tightly—he hadn't let go since the discovery of the portal. I had naïvely thought that all our problems would be solved the moment we saw the portal, but when had anything been that simple? Especially when it came to the supernatural—there was always an unexpected cost, a trick, a hidden motive.

This was just a small setback, I reassured myself. *It happens all the time.*

It just didn't usually happen when my children were involved.

I heard the crackle of a radio. Corrine had stopped spelling the portal and was trying to get into contact with the other team.

"Mona? Mona? Can you hear me?" she asked over the waves.

"I can hear you—everything okay?" Mona's voice sounded unnaturally high over the radio. "Anything happened yet?"

"No," Corrine replied, "it's not budging. I've tried everything I can think of."

There was silence over the line, and I looked worriedly up at Corrine. She shrugged.

"Okay," she replied. "At least we've found it—that's good news. Now we just have to find a way to get it open."

I could hear the determination in her voice, and smiled. We really needed a bit of perspective—it *was* good news. "Has it got a cover over it, like a translucent cover?" Mona asked.

"No. It's like black tar—looks almost like a live organism… seems to be moving of its own accord."

"I've never heard of anything like that," Mona replied faintly. "Don't touch it. We'll come over to you, we might have better luck shifting it if there's more of us."

Corrine nodded. "Okay—meet us on the mainland and we'll regroup." She cut the radio and turned to me, her expression as disappointed as I was sure mine was. "I just can't figure out how this has happened," she said. "Unused portals have been known to get a bit sticky with age, but I've never seen anything like *this*." She peered back down into the portal, and we both watched the hypnotic movements of the tar. I could see why Mona had advised us not to touch it—it looked like it would swallow us whole, like quicksand. It wasn't an appealing thought.

"Let's get back," Corrine murmured eventually. "Mona and the others will be there soon."

The plane changed direction, and soon we were hurtling back to the mainland.

"Do you think it could be spelled by witches?" Caleb asked Corrine.

She shook her head. "I doubt it – I'd be able to tell."

We were silent the rest of the way back, all of us looking out of the sea plane windows, watching the endless ocean—all racking our brains as to what, or who, could have caused a portal to get blocked in that way.

I was glad that we'd found it, but wished it didn't throw up more questions than it answered. I also had an overwhelmingly ominous feeling... what kind of dimension might our children be locked in?

TEJUS

Ash and Julian were bent over the sofa, attending to the small human girl. Hazel remained in the corner, sitting among the debris, still wearing the bedsheet clutched to her tightly.

What had I done?

I still couldn't comprehend how it had happened. The minister had told me that it was the marriage ceremony that created the change, a specific part of the marriage ceremony. How could he have got it so wrong? He had claimed it was the moment that the body, mind and soul were declared as one. I had assumed he meant theoretically—that the words and ritual of the ceremony would somehow make that true. Obviously I had been wrong, but did that mean that Hazel and I had become literally joined somehow? That she was as much a part of me as I felt I was of her?

There was no denying that I had felt something shift inside me—a moment when she had looked up at me, her eyes clear and honest as they met mine, and I'd felt myself mentally pour into her, holding nothing back. Was the transformation as simple as that?

Does it even matter?

I had ruined her. How would she love me now, when she had become a mind-hungry leech, all because she'd fallen for the wrong man—the wrong species? I felt morally bankrupt. Not only did I feel corrupt, but I felt like I had corrupted another, someone who was inherently good. The only creature I had ever learned to love more than myself.

I can't bear it to be this way...

I strode toward her, but she scurried up to her feet, desperately warning me back. I knew she wanted me to, but I couldn't just let her sit there, feeling like she was all alone in dealing with this.

Before I could touch her, she dashed past me, running into my bedroom and slamming the door shut. The others looked up in surprise, but I barely registered their glances. It was only when Ruby, coming down from the tower, tugged on my robe to get my attention and then scowled at me while gesturing to the slammed door, that I felt I should try to explain something.

Ruby shoved a piece of paper and some lead in my direction.

I hastily scribbled down the best I could, 'You need to speak to her—when you can. I'm sorry.'

Ruby snatched back the paper and rolled her eyes at me. I didn't know what else to say, and in all honesty I was sick of this farce. I wanted them all to leave.

Ruby tried to open the door, but Hazel had locked it from the inside. She struggled for a few moments and then gave up, slumping against it, dejected. Ash gallantly went to her side, and I turned away.

I was about to order them out when the small human groaned. She struggled up on the sofa and looked around the room, noticing the devastation that Benedict had caused with wide eyes.

"What happened?" she asked croakily.

It's over.

I sighed with relief. The final plague was over. I didn't know what this would mean in terms of the entity's rise, but for now I was grateful that Hellswan had survived it – barely.

The others all started talking at once, Ash trying to reassure Ruby, and Julian trying to explain to the young girl that it would all be all right.

"Tejus, what is going on with Hazel?" Ruby asked me, cutting through the noise. Everyone fell silent.

"I'm afraid you're going to have to wait until she wishes to tell you."

"What did you do to her?" she yelled, her cheeks heating up as she glared at me.

I turned toward the tower. I wanted to get away from them—I didn't need Ruby's judgment adding to the guilt I already felt. I needed to speak to Hazel alone, to tell her that the cravings would eventually pass, that she would in part return to normal…as normal as she could now be.

"Don't leave!" Ruby bit out. "I want to get to the bottom of this, and my friend's not speaking to me. I need answers *now*, sentry."

I bit my tongue. I had no idea what to say, and it

certainly wasn't my place to tell them about Hazel's transformation. I wasn't sure I would even know where to begin…

"You have to wait," I snapped.

"What about the stone?" the small human asked, breaking the brief silence that followed. "What happens now that Benedict—the entity—has taken another one?"

"And the apocalyptic signs are finished," Ruby whispered. "What does that mean?"

It occurred to me that I had never felt more responsible for the people of Hellswan and the humans in my care—and never felt more at a loss as to how I could fulfill that responsibility, now that I was no longer king.

"I don't know what it means. The material Hazel and I read indicated that the apocalyptic signs were just a warning system—not that it automatically meant the entity would rise…but the ministers have been wrong in the past," I murmured.

Very wrong.

"Why don't you know?" the human replied angrily. "You're the king, you should know some of this! How are you supposed to protect your kingdom and all your people if you don't know *any* of this?"

I couldn't help the smirk that twitched across my face.

"Actually, I'm not the king—Ash is."

The bewildered silence that greeted my remark was satisfying. Ash's paling, disbelieving face turned to mine.

"What?" he asked.

My smile faded. I didn't exactly like Ash, but I was handing him more of a curse than a blessing. For a moment I questioned my decision—was this boy able to rule Hellswan?

"You heard me," I retorted.

"I did," he replied slowly, "but I want to hear it again—and know what you mean."

The bafflement of his expression had turned into determination. I remembered why I had thought Ash would be capable. He wouldn't be plagued with the uncertainty I had faced, the burden of my family's name. He would rule with fresh eyes—a mind that was less jaded than mine.

"You need to discuss it with the ministers," I replied. "It is best that they induct you. Although, take the advice of ministers with caution. Memenion will be helpful to you also, should you need it."

I strode over to the door of my living room and held it

open. Enough was enough.

"And I'm afraid that is all I can tell you. Please leave—I want to be alone with Hazel."

"I'm not sure you should be," Ruby muttered, glancing balefully in my direction.

Eventually they left. Ash walked out in a daze, with Ruby almost having to guide him to the hallway. I shut the door when the last one was out.

"Hazel?" I called as softly as I could through the bedroom door.

Only silence greeted me.

ASH

"I don't understand why he couldn't give me more answers than that," I muttered to Ruby as we made our way down from Tejus's tower. "It's not like the ministers are exactly forthcoming."

She took my hand, nodding along with my complaints, but a small smile crept across her face.

"What?" I asked.

"Aren't you excited?" she asked, squeezing my hand.

I returned her smile. "Honestly, Shortie? I'm terrified."

"You don't need to be," she said. "Well…maybe for the trials…" She trailed off, and I could practically see her brain going into overdrive.

"Stop worrying." I laughed at her.

"You started it. I *was* excited for you…"

We entered the belly of the castle, and things seemed to have calmed down. The ministers were no longer behaving like headless birds, but now it was worse. Every time we passed one of them, they would stare at me, eyes practically popping out of their skulls as they looked me up and down, and then took in the group of humans behind me.

"Why aren't you speaking to them?" Ruby whispered as we passed another pair of ministers.

"I want to find some I know better…most of these ministers don't know their ass from their elbow."

"Do you think any of them really knows what's going on?" she asked.

"Nope." I grinned. "Maybe that will work to my advantage."

We turned a corner in the main hallway; I was trying to find my way to the main council room, hoping that I would find Qentos. He was possibly the world's biggest fool, but he also seemed honest…as far as ministers went.

"Ashbik?" Lieutenant Ragnhild stood in our path, smiling pleasantly at our group. Now that Commander Varga was gone, I supposed Ragnhild was left in charge of the guards. I had never really spoken to him—he was quiet, kept to himself, and didn't really socialize with any of the other guards in the mess hall. I didn't know if that was because he was naturally shy, or because he was just stuck-up.

I guess I'm going to find out.

"Lieutenant Ragnhild," I acknowledged. "Can I help you?"

"I bring word from the ministers. May I speak freely?" he asked, looking at Ruby and then over to the rest of the humans.

"Yes."

"Very well. The internal ministers of Hellswan have agreed that you are to be named king, but we will need to clear the decision with the Impartial Ministers—we will need their say-so before the coronation can take place, and before you are permitted to take part in the Imperial trials."

I swallowed.

This is too much…

"Thank you, Lieutenant," I managed.

Ragnhild made a move to leave. Tradition would have me as a servant bow to him, and him bow to me as a king. But I was not either of those things at the moment…

I offered him my hand, and he shook it, relieved.

"Ashbik, you should know"—he hesitated, glancing around the hallway— "not all want you in power…you will have enemies within the ministry. Might I suggest that you deal with them swiftly? Know that I am at your service."

This time my thanks were genuine.

I had always known from the beginning that if I were ever to succeed to the throne, there would be many within the ministry who would not want me there. I would have to watch my back…though I had expected that threat to come from the Hellswan family themselves.

Ragnhild left, and we changed course, going back to the human quarters. I didn't really know where else to go. If the ministers needed to find me, they knew where to look.

"That doesn't sound good," Ruby whispered as we continued down the corridor.

"Don't worry. I always knew that would be the deal. I've also got a few more supporters than I thought I would have," I replied, looking straight at her.

She smiled, but I could tell her mind was elsewhere.

"Are you thinking about the trials?" I asked.

"Queen Trina."

I shot Ruby a reassuring smile, but if I was perfectly honest with myself I was worried about that too. I had seen the power that she had shown during the trials so far, and the woman was deadly. Fast, vicious, determined. Sometimes I had wondered if she was receiving help from the Impartial Ministers. She always seemed to be prepared, even when the others weren't. The only time I had seen her truly affected was after the first trial, where they had taken the hallucinogens. I had no idea whose beating heart she had gripped in her fist, but it had hurt her. Badly.

Originally, I had turned a blind eye. I hadn't wanted to believe that she was getting help from them—all I had cared about was bringing the Hellswan rule to an end. Now my primary goal would be keeping her out of power.

"Ashbik?"

I heard the quivering voice of Qentos behind me, and turned to face him. Lithan was at his side, his beady little eyes fixed on my hand holding Ruby's.

"Yes?" I retorted. They had already started to irritate me.

"I take it you've h-heard the good news?" stuttered Qentos. "We are to take you to the Impartial Ministers at dawn…you should…look the part."

The sentry was actually starting to sweat now, and I took pity on him.

"I'll wear the right robes, Qentos."

Jenney will have to swipe some for me...

"The other kings and Queen Trina will also have an opinion on this," snapped Lithan. "I doubt that Queen Trina will agree, to be honest."

"Maybe," I agreed mildly, knowing that it would infuriate Lithan.

He glared at me. "You should be more concerned than that—she holds substantial sway over the Impartial Ministers."

I knew that, and I didn't need Lithan's reminder. But I also knew that Queen Trina had been concerned about coming up against Tejus in the trials—she thought he was a worthy opponent, whereas I had a feeling that she would underestimate me. That would work to my advantage.

"Maybe," I agreed again, smiling at Lithan. "Maybe not."

My words had the desired effect, and Lithan turned away from me in disgust.

"We will need Tejus to attend too," muttered Qentos as he watched the departing figure of his fellow minister. "He hasn't yet explained himself to the Impartial Ministers...they will have a lot to say about this, a lot to say!"

"I'll see you later, Qentos," I replied, wanting to leave the sentry to his own panic. I had enough of my own to deal with.

Ruby and I carried on to the human quarters, both of us silent for a while as we observed more horrified and confused looks from passing ministers.

"I really need to get them replaced," I muttered.

"Qentos and Lithan, or the entire lot of them?" Ruby replied with a grin. "I'm totally behind either decision."

I laughed. "Lithan and Qentos for now…maybe the others later."

I was joking about it with Ruby, but I meant every word. If Lithan was against me, then he would be a problem—a dangerous one. Whether Qentos was on my side or not was irrelevant. He was weak, and would side with Lithan on all matters. The only problem was, I didn't know who else I could trust in the current Hellswan ministry. I didn't trust Tejus's judgment on the matter either. Like most people who had been brought up in the seat of power, Tejus always felt he could rule by force—I didn't think he'd even considered the idea that his ministers might not be behind his every rule and decision.

Maybe I could get rid of them all?

The idea was tempting, but I wasn't going to seriously

consider it—not yet. I was far from wielding that kind of power. Right now, I was still seen as a kitchen boy.

"I think you're going to be great, by the way." Ruby looked at me sideways, a small smile playing on her lips.

"At being king?"

"King and emperor. I know you can do it, Ash. You're the most impressive sentry I know."

"You don't know that many sentries," I pointed out.

"I know enough," she rebuked. "You've wanted this ever since you were a kid. Don't let Queen Trina or anyone else get in the way—this is your chance."

The fact that she believed I could survive the trials and knock Queen Trina out of the running was humbling, but I couldn't quite share her optimism. Tejus had been wounded so badly that he'd had to step down. That didn't exactly fill me with confidence. Before the kingship trials, I'd believed that I could beat him—not easily, but that it would be possible. After hearing and seeing all that he'd faced in the trials and within his own kingdom with the entity, Tejus had gone up in my estimation, and I felt like I paled in comparison.

"I feel like I already had my chance, and I blew it," I replied, thinking of the kingship trials.

"*I* blew it, remember?" Ruby replied earnestly. "I'm starting to think that Benedict might have sucked my energy dry the night before the trials—it would explain why I had none for you to syphon off, and why I woke up alone in a random hallway of the castle. Creepy, right?"

"Right," I muttered darkly. It was more than creepy—it made me incensed with rage that the entity had harmed Ruby in that way, and used her friend to do it. She was putting on a brave face now, but I remembered how devastated she'd been after the disk trials…and that kiss.

"Why are you smiling?" she asked curiously.

"Nothing. Just… remembering."

"Remembering what?"

"When I look back on that day, it's not really the trial I remember—it's *you*."

I pulled her body toward mine, sliding my hands around her waist. I didn't care that we were out in the middle of the hallway, and I no longer paid attention to the disbelieving looks of the ministers.

"Ash, we're in…"

"I don't care," I interjected.

"Okay," she breathed as I lowered my mouth to hers. She lifted up on her tiptoes, and our lips met. It was a chaste kiss, but it was enough—enough to make me want to carry Ruby off to a room somewhere and let the trials, the ministers, the kings, the crowns, everything continue without me. If I could remain in Ruby's arms, then that would be enough for me. It would be enough for anyone—kitchen boy or king.

"Come on." She smiled dozily at me. "We need to get Jenney to steal you some appropriate clothes."

I laughed against her forehead. "How do you know I don't have any?"

"I just do—unless you're planning on wearing an apron."

"It's tempting. It would really give the ministers something to stare at," I mused.

"If that's your only game plan, then I have a much better way of getting those results…"

Ruby pulled on the collar of my shirt, bringing me down toward her. She kissed me again, more deeply this time, her tongue nudging against mine and her hands winding around my neck.

I was too entranced to notice, but I think we put on quite a show.

HAZEL

When the raised voices had died down, I leaned back against the bedframe in relief. I'd hated shutting Ruby out—literally—but I didn't know how to tell her what had happened. I knew I would eventually, but I just couldn't make sense of it myself yet. Honestly, I didn't know if I'd ever be able to fully make sense of it. Now that the initial shock had sort of died down, other realities reared up to face me. How was I going to explain this to my mom and dad? What would happen when I returned to The Shade— would I be a danger to people? Also, more immediately, had Tejus *known* this would happen? Was this why he had asked me to stay away? And if so, why the *hell* hadn't he warned me explicitly?

I recalled the shocked expression he'd exhibited when I first started syphoning off him. Perhaps he hadn't expected it exactly, but the look of horror that had replaced it kind of indicated to me that he had known *what* had happened almost immediately.

Reluctantly, I accepted the fact that I needed to speak to Tejus. Hopefully he could answer some of my questions—and if he couldn't, then I would make damn sure that he got the answers from somewhere.

I looked around the room, trying to locate my clothing. I found my pants and shirt, and then the black robe I'd been wearing for warmth. I wanted a bath, desperately, but I wanted answers more. Comfort would have to wait.

The hunger I was feeling had settled down into a dull ache ever since I'd been alone in the room. I expected that it would flare up again as soon as I got close to Tejus, but I was ready for it. I would have to learn to control it, or spend the rest of my days avoiding my friends and family in case I sucked their energy totally dry. I wondered if this was what it felt like to be a baby vamp... I'd witnessed the insatiable hunger that those new to the lifestyle experienced, and this didn't seem much different. There didn't seem to be enough energy in the world to satisfy me. I could only hope that, like vamps' hunger for blood, it would fade over time—and that I would learn to control it, just like Tejus did.

Slowly, cautiously, I opened the door to the bedroom.

Tejus was sitting on the sofa, head in hands, surrounded by the devastation that Benedict had caused. The lights of the stones in the lock cast the room in ever-changing colors, suffusing with the soft light coming from outside—dawn could only be a few hours away. It had been a *long* night.

My instant reaction was to fly into Tejus's arms to find comfort. It wasn't a good idea. Not after what had happened last time. And I could already feel the hunger tugging at the corners of my mind, making me feel hollow inside and desperate to be filled.

Tejus turned to face me, his face bleak and gray. The sharp, distinct lines of his face seemed to be etched deeper, the hollows under his cheekbones more pronounced than I'd ever seen. Dark circles shadowed his eyes, and I was once again reminded of the damage that the last trial had caused him, both physically and mentally.

I wasn't the only one suffering.

"I'm so sorry, Hazel."

His voice was hoarse and broken. It hurt me to hear it.

"Forgive me. I didn't know that it could happen that way," he continued.

Happen that way?

I stayed silent, waiting for him to elaborate. I felt the old distance seeping in between us—and the worst thing was that I felt powerless to stop it.

"I had heard a rumor, an old tale really, that when a sentry married outside their species, the non-sentry would transform into…one of us. I half-believed it, and checked with a minister to see if it was true. He told me that it was—that part of the marriage ceremony bonded the couple in a certain way. It was why I told you to stay away." His breath hitched. "I didn't want this for you."

He dragged his hands through his hair, his expression tortured.

"I-I don't understand," I stuttered. "Why didn't you *say* anything?"

"I knew that you loved me. I didn't want you to have to make that choice. I knew you had a life mapped out for yourself—one that didn't include me or Nevertide. And then… I couldn't bear for you to choose your life, and destroy mine by leaving."

It was selfish of him – taking away my choices like that, but I couldn't say he didn't warn me about that aspect of his character. He had warned me time and time again, and I had ignored him, I had loved him anyway and not taken no for an answer.

Where does that leave me now?

Still in love with him.

I'm an idiot.

"You had no right to make that choice for me. You should have told me—even if you thought it was just a marriage ceremony, you should have said *something*. You *knew* there was a chance something like this could happen."

"I know."

"And you did it anyway."

"Yes."

At least he was honest.

When he looked up at me, I could hardly meet his eyes. There was so much sorrow in them—only a few hours ago they had been looking up at me from bed, sparkling. Now they were black, endless wells of misery.

"I... I have fallen in love with you, Hazel," he stated, calmly. "It was never my intention—I tried to protect you."

"But you don't know how to! You treat me like I'm incapable of making up my own mind! And now you'll never know—you'll never know if, despite knowing what I would lose, I would still have chosen you."

Would I?

I didn't know anymore. I couldn't see the choice clearly. I felt like he hadn't trusted me enough to love him back, not really – he hadn't trusted me to make the choice on my own. Now all I felt was a raging *need* for his energy, and for the past few hours to be completely wiped away—for me to be back entwined in his limbs, his body touching mine.

The fight went out of me.

I wasn't sure I entirely liked what I had become, but there was no point trying to pretend that if he *had* given me the choice I would have completely dismissed the chance of a future together...

"What happens now?" I asked. "The hunger—does it remain like this? Will I always feel this way?"

"No. It will fade. I'll help you overcome this, Hazel – I

promise."

"And when will I be able to be around my friends?"

"It might take some time to be near them without wanting to syphon off them. You need to learn how to control your urges. We can practice. You can use me."

"Not without hurting you, I can't," I pointed out.

"You'll learn."

I was hesitant to accept his offer. I at least wanted to wait till he was back to full health—Tejus himself had told me that sentries had rapid healing powers, but as far as I could see, he hadn't recovered from the ghoul attack yet.

"When Benedict came into the room, he tried to syphon off you and then stopped, like your energy wasn't strong enough. What was that about?"

"I'm still not healed."

"But you must have more energy than someone like Yelena. She's only a kid."

"Children are often more potent—that's why many of the humans captured from Earth were young. It makes sense that Benedict would choose her, especially as he has syphoned off her before. As you know, it makes the process easier the second time around."

I nodded, understanding, but it still felt like he wasn't telling me the full story.

"I don't know why I'm still wounded," he continued. "I was certain that Queen Trina was harmed by the ghouls, but she seemed fine at the meeting. It's infuriating."

His jaw tightened, and he glared down at the floor.

"Is there anyone you can see? I know you didn't want to get the ministers involved earlier, but maybe it's a good idea?"

Tejus grimaced.

"They're not actually *my* ministers anymore. No doubt one of them could take a look, but I really don't think they'll be able to help. It will go away in time—like your hunger."

Nice diversion.

Clearly Tejus no longer wanted to talk about his injury. I also knew from experience that there would be no way I could force him to.

"Maybe tomorrow I'll try syphoning." I swallowed. It was difficult for me to get the words out—to try to restrain myself when all I wanted to do was drain him.

Tejus stood up from the sofa, and I backed up against the bedroom entrance.

"Don't come closer, Tejus," I warned.

"Trust me."

He took the few steps across the room to reach me. He came to a stop about a foot away from me, staring down, his eyes calmer but no less troubled. The desire to syphon off him was starting to grow intolerable. A tingling spread across my body, as if every cell was reacting to my need for Tejus's energy.

"Trust me," he repeated.

But you don't trust me.

"I can't!" I cried, feeling the flicker of my mind as it snaked toward his—I wouldn't permit myself to make whatever the ghouls had done to him any worse. I jerked backward, wrapping my arms around myself. "Please just leave. I'm worried I'm going to hurt you – I should be alone."

"I don't think that's a good idea," he retorted.

"I don't care—it's what's happening." I stepped back into the bedroom, slamming the door shut behind me and locking it.

I might not like what I'd become, but Tejus was right about one thing—I needed to learn to control it. I wasn't going to lose myself in my newfound sentry powers, and I wasn't going to let it alienate me from my friends. If that happened, Nevertide would have beaten me—and there was no *way in hell* that was going to happen.

Tejus

"Are you ready, King Tejus?" A guard appeared at the door to the living room, staring in barely concealed astonishment at the whirlwind of devastation that Benedict had left in his wake.

I nodded. "Wait in the hallway," I commanded.

I walked back to the bedroom door and knocked. It had been an hour since Hazel had disappeared into it, and I hadn't heard a thing from her since.

"Hazel?" I called.

I hoped she was sleeping, but after a pause, a wavering voice replied.

"Yes?"

"I need to go with Ash to the pavilion. There will be guards stationed outside your door. Let them know if you need anything."

"Okay," came the reply.

"Can I get you anything before I leave?" I asked.

"I'm fine – I'm just…a bit freaked out. Go… I'll be okay."

I waited for a few moments, leaning my head on the doorframe. I hoped that she would come out, but she made no further sound as I left. Despite what I wanted to do, giving her some space to process everything was probably the best course of action…and it didn't look like I had much choice in the matter anyway.

When I reached the courtyard the guard left me, and I stood opposite Lithan and Qentos who were waiting with four vultures.

"Where's Ash?" I asked curtly.

"On his way," replied Lithan with a malicious smile. "No doubt finishing up some kitchen duties."

"Careful, Lithan. In a few short hours, Ash will be your king—and I hope for your sake, you find a more dignified manner with which to address him."

"We shall see about that," he retorted.

"Ah. I suppose you hope that Queen Trina will stand in the way of his coronation? You're a fool, Lithan. Queen Trina wants to rise to power—she'll see this as a blessing."

Lithan's face fell. I would enjoy watching Lithan's political desires sink into the gutter—it might be one of the very few things I would enjoy after giving up the crown.

"Tejus."

Ash appeared in the entranceway to the castle.

"Ash," I replied courteously, noticing the red robe he was wearing, no doubt stolen from my or Jenus's wardrobe. Jenney was obviously proving to be an effective ally.

Good, I thought. He was going to need all the help he could get.

"Let's not keep the Impartial Ministers waiting." Ash addressed Qentos and Lithan. I hid a smirk, and mounted my vulture. I wondered how much time it would take Ash to reorder the Hellswan ministry once the entity was re-imprisoned…I didn't imagine it would be long.

We flew to the pavilion, chasing the early dawn. When we arrived, the Impartial Ministers and the remaining champions were already there and waiting. Even from this distance, I could sense the glee spewing forth from Queen Trina.

The four of us approached the pavilion. As soon as we were close, Ash started to shake, his eyes fixed on the queen. Glancing up at his face, I saw it was blind rage that was causing his reaction—and if he wasn't careful, Ash was going to blow his chances.

"Steady," I murmured, pulling on his robe. "There's going to be another opportunity—remember what you're here for."

"I want her dead," he growled.

"You're not the only one," I replied, nodding in Memenion's direction. "But right now you're at the mercy of the Impartial Ministers, so pull yourself together."

Ash straightened his robe and nodded curtly in understanding as we walked up the stone steps of the Pavilion. The Impartial Ministers eyed him warily—clearly word had already gotten around.

"King Tejus, what is the meaning of this?" one of the Impartial Ministers barked at me. I smiled back, knowing full well what their response was going to be. I had put them in a near impossible situation, and it was unlikely they would reject Ash's bid for kingship. If they wanted the trials to continue, then they needed him.

"I have abdicated from the throne, and nominate Ash in my place. The true winner of the trials." Amidst the uproar that greeted my announcement, I continued to explain about Hazel and the stone from the entity lock.

"But it is a mistake then!" one of the ministers blustered. "We cannot hold you accountable for that."

"*I* hold myself accountable, and do not believe my crown was rightfully won."

The group fell silent as Queen Trina's laughter pierced the air.

"This is too wonderful!" she exclaimed. "The brave, gallant Tejus giving up his crown so the kitchen boy gets his day in the sun!"

I ignored her after sending a warning glance to Ash, ensuring he did the same. The Impartial Ministers looked around the pavilion, clearly waiting for another royal to step forward and object.

"He was Queen Trina Seraq's advisor," one of the ministers burst out after both Memenion and Hadalix remained silent. "I'm not entirely sure that is permissible—especially as he will be entered into the

Imperial trials!"

"I have no objection. Do you, Hadalix?" Memenion asked the other king.

Hadalix looked confused, and suspicious, but shook his head. "No...I don't think I have any objections."

"And clearly Queen Trina doesn't." Memenion rolled his eyes.

The Impartial Ministers started to mutter amongst themselves, and Ash glanced at me, his features tense.

I looked over at Memenion, who nodded slowly in my direction. It seemed like my plan was going to work...as long as the ministers couldn't come up with anymore objections.

Their huddle ended, and my heart sank as I regarded their smug expressions.

They've found an excuse.

"Do forgive us, Ashbik," one of them whined in a nasal voice, "but we are not entirely sure of the kingdom's safety in the hands of someone who has had no political experience in the past." He held up a hand to stop Ash interrupting. "However, your success in the trials can't be ignored."

The minister smiled at me.

"There was also another who was entered into the trials who may have been affected by this stone of yours, and that is your brother, Jenus Hellswan. We would like him to be brought out of banishment, and they will compete for the Hellswan crown—a little unprecedented, but it has been done before."

Oh, hell no.

My brother. Of course.

I should have anticipated this.

"You want me to bring Jenus out of banishment?" I hissed. "He is a danger to the Hellswan kingdom and has never been anything less. You are making a mistake."

"We don't *want* you to, Tejus. As an abdicator of the throne, you no longer have the power to refuse us. We are *commanding* you to do so."

I kept myself from reacting further, though it took all my willpower to keep my fists at my side. Ash chose to show no such restraint.

"Are you mad?" he cried.

"Ash," I snapped. "Let the Impartial Ministers have their way if it so pleases them. What do you propose to do, put them through another trial?" I asked the minister through gritted teeth.

"Exactly that. Ashbik and Jenus will compete for the crown, and the winner shall be put through to the Imperial trials. I don't believe you can ask for more benevolence than that, surely?"

"It is *very* generous of you," I replied, my voice drenched in sarcasm.

"Then we will reconvene here at dusk. The trial will commence then—I take it that will give you enough time?" the minister asked, his veneer of faux politeness as practiced as mine.

"Of course."

"Very well then."

The Impartial Ministers all exited the pavilion together, and I leant back against one of the arches, feeling completely powerless. My brother returning as the entity rose to power was a deadly combination...Hellswan could not afford more enemies within its walls.

"I have the feeling this has backfired somewhat," commented Memenion as he approached Ash and me.

"They always find a way." I sighed. "It just infuriates me that they can't see the danger in returning Jenus from banishment. Who knows what evil flows through my brother's mind? What form his revenge will take?"

Memenion sighed.

"I imagine they believe that you alone will be his enemy—the one who will have to bear the brunt of his wrath. In their mind, I imagine it is a win-win situation. Clearly they don't know what he is capable of."

I agreed with Memenion—that was probably what the fools thought, but I knew my brother and I knew his temper. I wasn't afraid for myself. I had been coming up against Jenus for years. It was Hazel I was concerned about, and what might happen to her friends were my brother to gain power.

"He won't get the chance," Ash grumbled. "I won't let him."

I nodded, hoping that Ash's rage toward my brother would be more of an incentive to beat him in the trials. I hadn't forgotten that it was Jenus who had locked Ruby up in a cellar, and I was sure Ash hadn't either.

"Let's get going. If we're going to reach him before sundown we need to hurry—I want to stop at the castle first."

Ash and I left the pavilion, followed by Lithan and Qentos. The former was barely bothering to try to hide his delight at the outcome of the meeting. When we reached the birds, I commanded Lithan and Qentos to go on ahead—I'd had enough of their company for one day.

"Why did you keep Lithan on after your father's death?" Ash asked, as the ministers' birds rose up into the sky.

"Keep your friends close, and your enemies closer. If you rule in a kingdom where you are loathed, it is better that the men who intend to stab you in the back are kept in sight at all times."

Ash looked surprised at my declaration, and I laughed.

"Did you think I didn't know that I was hated?" I asked.

He looked at me for a few moments, as if trying to comprehend something that was a great mystery to him.

"Why are you doing this?" he asked after a pause.

I smiled.

"I know you think the worst of me, Ash. Perhaps rightly. But please believe me when I say that I have always tried to put the interests of Hellswan and Nevertide first. I want what is best for this land—and at the moment, that means the entity being stopped and Queen Trina staying well away from the seat of power."

"And you think I am the best choice to accomplish that?" he asked skeptically.

Yes.

"You are a viable option," I retorted.

Ash burst out laughing. "Right." He nodded. "A viable option. And this has nothing to do with Hazel?"

"What do you mean?" I frowned.

Ash smiled in an irritating fashion. "I just thought that maybe she had an opinion on you becoming emperor. An opinion that was so strong it may have swayed you."

"Don't be ridiculous," I snapped. "We need to get going."

"What's up with her anyway?" he probed as we prepared the birds.

"Nothing I'm willing to discuss with you. You're not king yet, kitchen boy."

We flew back to the castle. Jenus's location was out by the borders of Hellswan, but I felt it would be a better idea to take bull-horses than vultures. Jenus would be weak, but it was better not to risk him mind-controlling a bird mid-flight on our return to the pavilion. This would mean leaving Hazel alone in the castle for more time than I would like. I felt it wouldn't be long till the hunger got to her, and if she lost her control around her friends, she would never forgive herself…or me.

RUBY

I had tried to keep myself busy. I had spent about an hour rearranging and changing all the bedding for the kids, finding more suitable locations for them to sleep, locations that would mean they weren't constantly sleeping in the living room. It meant that I was now sharing my room with two others, but that didn't matter much at the moment—it wasn't like I was getting much sleep anyway.

According to Jenney, the kids had livened up a bit ever since Benedict had been possessed completely by the entity and had vanished off to the temple where Hazel said he was trapped. It made me feel slightly nauseous that he had obviously been syphoning off them while they slept with none of us ever knowing. Now the kids kept mainly to themselves, spending most of their time in the servants' quarters or in the garden outside during the day, avoiding the castle as best they could. I was hugely grateful for Jenney—without her, they would have been completely abandoned in this strange place, and I doubted that many of them would be dealing with it as well as Yelena. She was a *weird* kid, but weird was clearly what was needed around here to survive.

I had just finished putting her to bed—it was morning now, but she hadn't slept much either in the last few days, and she looked exhausted. Julian wasn't really looking any better, so I had given him strict instructions to do the same. After moaning that I was treating him like a kid, mid-yawn he had closed his eyes and a moment later had started snoring.

Jenney came into the living room with yet another pile of fresh laundry.

"Thanks, Jenney." I smiled. "Are the kids downstairs?"

"Yes—they're in one of the old abandoned rooms, complaining that they don't have 'Internet'…does that mean anything to you?"

I laughed. "Yeah."

"Well…" She shrugged, and dumped the laundry down on one of the less cluttered sofas. "I'm going to get them something to eat. Do you want anything?"

"Maybe later."

She was halfway to the door when she turned around and gave me a reassuring smile.

"Ruby, Ash is going to be fine. You know how stubborn he is—he's not going to let this chance slip away from him."

I groaned. "It's his stubbornness that worries me. He won't give up—and that means that he's going to try to outdo himself in the trials to prove his worth, and if the kingship trials were anything to go by, it's going to be dangerous."

"He's lived in Hellswan all his life—he knows danger. And he knows how to survive. You're just going to worry yourself sick if you keep thinking about it."

"I know." I sighed. "I'm trying to keep busy but…anyway, they'll be back soon, right?"

"Right," Jenney confirmed. "I'll see you later. Stay calm."

I nodded, leaning back against the sofa. I could stay

calm. Jenney left and I looked over at the windows. Dawn had long passed and now the morning sun was shining as brightly as it ever did in Nevertide, which wasn't much. The peace was kind of unnerving. The apocalyptic signs were over, and apart from Benedict coming to take another stone, it felt like we were on pause, waiting for the entity to come—waiting for the destruction of Hellswan and all the other kingdoms to commence.

I shifted on the sofa, trying to get comfortable, and heard the crumple of paper in the pocket of my robe.

The letter.

I reached inside and pulled it out. I stared down at the handwritten scrawl of my name, thinking how strange it was to be looking at a dead man's penmanship. I turned it over, about to open it, when the main door swung open.

Hazel stood in the doorway, her arms wrapped around her, but this time she was dressed properly, and her eyes no longer looked as wild and unhinged as I'd seen them earlier.

"Oh, Hazel, thank God! Are you okay?" I shoved the letter back inside my robe and hurried over to her. Before I could get close, she held her arm out, warning me back.

"Wait! Ruby, I need you to...hang back, okay?" she

replied in a wobbly, scratchy voice. "There's something I need to tell you, and it's not good…and I just need some space while I try to get it out."

"Okay," I replied slowly, not having the faintest idea what was going on. I'd never seen Hazel like this. She could be a little dramatic sometimes, but this wasn't like that—something had clearly scared the living daylights out of her, but other than Benedict, I couldn't really imagine what that was.

She was silent, watching me take a few steps back.

"The suspense is killing me," I said, trying to lighten the mood, but clearly not doing a very good job of it.

"I'm sorry. It's difficult…" She twisted her fingers around one another as she stood there, like she was waiting for a firing squad. "I got… kind of intimate with Tejus last night…and now…" She swallowed hard. "N-Now I'm a sentry."

"What?" I burst out, half wanting to laugh.

"Yeah…a sentry. Turns out, the powers are transferable." She gulped.

"Hazel, you're not a sentry—of course you're not. That's…*impossible!* What makes you think that?"

Had my friend gone completely mad?

"The fact that I started to syphon off Tejus was the first clue." She smiled weakly.

What the heck...

"Okay. You need to explain—from the beginning."

Hazel nodded, but remained standing where she was, eyeing me nervously.

"And you're starting to freak me out, so can you please come and sit down?" I gestured to the sofas, going to perch on the end of one myself—it kind of felt like my legs weren't going to hold me up much longer.

Hazel looked at the sofa and then at me. She nodded, and then walked slowly, coming to sit on the sofa that faced mine.

"This has happened before," she breathed. "Tejus told me...but it was different...it was the marriage ceremony—it wasn't meant to happen like this..."

I waited for her to take another deep breath, and then I interrupted. "You're really not making any sense!"

"Sorry—I'm just..." She ran her hands through her hair, and I noticed they were shaking. "I'm crazy—I feel like I'm going *crazy*."

She took another deep breath and then finally started to tell me the story. I sat there with my mouth open, disbelieving and overwhelmed in equal measure...and mostly thinking what a giant idiot Tejus was.

I leaned forward when she had finished, trying to touch her hand. She jumped backward on the sofa.

"Don't! You don't understand, Ruby—I'm so hungry." Her eyes widened. "And you're so...your energy is amazing—it's like—*glowing* or something..."

Hazel trailed off and I started to feel flutters at my temple. I looked at Hazel in shock, but it was like she was no longer seeing *me*, but what was *inside* of me. Suddenly I cried out as searing pain shot through my mind—like a migraine, only a thousand times worse, and similar to what Jenus had done in the storm cellar.

"STOP!" I yelled.

Instantly the pain receded, and Hazel jumped to her feet, staring at me in horror.

"Oh, my God, Ruby, I'm so sorry!" she blurted out, already backing up toward the door. "It just seems to happen! I'm losing control..."

"It's okay," I muttered, clutching my head in my hands. *Jeez,* it hurt. "Don't go anywhere—please." I gestured for her to sit back down, but had to wait a moment before I could look up at her. It felt like little elephants were dancing in my skull and the light was hurting my eyes.

"I'm so sorry," she whispered.

"It's not your fault. You can't help it," I replied, more for my own sake than hers. I really didn't want to get angry at Hazel—it was the last thing she needed. All the same, I couldn't help but wish she'd been a bit more cautious before jumping into bed with Tejus…I knew how she felt about him, but a bit of caution and fact-checking beforehand would have been good.

"Some first time, huh?" I half-smiled at her.

"Don't," she retorted. "I'm *definitely* not ready to laugh about it yet."

"Fair enough. So—the syphoning…can't you do it in a more…*gentle* way? Like Ash and Tejus can?" I asked hopefully.

"I would if I could, but I don't know how. Tejus says it will be something I learn. Being able to control the hunger will help, but I don't even know where to begin."

I nodded. "Maybe getting you some food would be a good place to start?"

"Yeah. I'm just trying to avoid bumping into anyone—I don't want to end up syphoning off one of the kids. I thought I might be safe with you, that I wouldn't allow myself to let it consume me, but…"

"But it was a dismal failure," I observed. "That's okay—baby steps…baby steps and annoying ministers maybe? I don't want to sound callous, but maybe there might be some of them you could practice on?"

I thought it was quite a good idea, but Hazel shook her head.

"You know I can't do that," she replied. "They'll lock me up or something until I learn some self-control."

"Ash would never allow that," I pointed out.

"*If* Ash becomes king."

"You knew about that?" I replied, surprised.

"I overheard Tejus telling the ministers."

Suddenly everything clicked into place. "Right—Tejus did something completely unselfish and you…"

"Yep."

"Okay." I nodded. Then, seeing Hazel's fed-up expression, I changed the subject. "Let's get you some food and I'll stop interrogating you."

"That would be nice."

Hazel's reply was sarcastic, and it gave me hope. She might be a sentry, or have a sentry's powers, but she was still first and foremost Hazel—Nevertide hadn't beaten her yet.

We made our way down to the servants' quarters, Hazel walking a few paces behind me to ensure that we didn't physically bump into anyone. We passed a couple of servants and Hazel backed up against the wall, staring down at the floor. When we got to the kitchen she stopped me.

"You go in first—make sure there's no one around," she hissed at me.

I peered around the partially open door. Only Jenney was standing at the stove, and I remembered that the kids were in one of the abandoned rooms.

"It's just Jenney," I replied. "Is that okay?"

Hazel deliberated for a few moments.

"I think so, as long as she keeps her distance. Other than Tejus, sentries don't seem to make me as hungry."

That made a little sense to me. If I was to think about it in comparison to vamps, they *could* drink off one another, but it never appealed the same way human blood did. Not even close.

We entered the kitchen, and Jenney waved at us distractedly from a boiling pot. "You hungry?" she asked us both. I looked at Hazel, who had gone back to clamping her arms around herself.

Well…one of us is.

"Food would be good—whatever you've got," I replied.

"Pitsa, actually."

What?

"Um…do you mean *pizza?*" I asked, looking at the boiling pot—it looked more like lumpy sentry stew to me.

"Right," Jenney agreed, mouthing the word silently. "The kids were explaining to me how to make it. This is for the ministers." She stirred the pot. "Give me a couple of minutes and the *pizza* will be right with you."

"Thanks!" I exclaimed. Hellswan was looking up.

Hazel drew up a chair at a table, as far away from Jenney and me as she could get.

While Jenney's attention was on the stove, I mouthed at Hazel, "We should tell her." Hazel looked pained, but after a couple of moments she nodded. She didn't look pleased by the idea, but I guessed eventually everyone would have to know. It wasn't like we were going to be able to keep it a secret.

I looked at Hazel expectantly, waiting for her to say something.

She sighed.

"Jenney, have you ever heard of a non-sentry becoming a sentry?" she asked.

Jenney chuckled, and continued stirring the pot.

"No...why? Are you looking to get comfy in Nevertide?" she replied, and then laughed at her own joke. When Hazel and I were silent, she spun around.

"What's going on?" she asked, all traces of amusement gone.

Between us we told her the whole story—skirting around Hazel and Tejus's intimacy, but it was implied. I thought that shocked Jenney more than anything else, but I didn't really know why.

"That's incredible," she breathed when we'd finished. Hazel looked uncomfortable, and I imagined it wouldn't be for the last time over the coming days...

"But you can't syphon safely right now?" she asked Hazel.

"No. It's horrible. I almost wiped out Tejus and then hurt Ruby," Hazel replied, shamefaced.

Jenney was silent for a few moments, looking thoughtful.

"That makes sense. When sentries are first born the kids have little or no control over who they syphon off, so they do it by accident all the time. Obviously, they're not as strong as an adult, so you hardly notice it. Just a mild headache. As they grow up, they learn. It really doesn't take that long. And as you're aware of it already, it will probably take even less time for you. I don't think this is going to affect you long term…not hugely, anyway."

As soon as Jenney finished her sentence, the door to the kitchen burst open and one of the kids came running in— the youngest one we had, a Portuguese boy called Carlito.

"Jenney, I hungry!" he cried in broken English. When he saw Hazel and me sitting at the table he smiled and waved, but his face fell when Hazel jerked back and closed her eyes.

"It's okay, Carlito. Hazel has a headache—head pain?" I checked the boy understood what I was saying. He looked confused, but nodded while heading back toward the door, clearly deciding that he no longer wanted to be in the kitchen.

When he was gone, Jenney and I turned to Hazel.

'That bad, huh?" I asked softly.

She nodded, looking down at the table.

Maybe we couldn't wait that long for Hazel to learn to get a grip on this.

"Okay, I think we need to try again," I announced. Hazel and Jenney both looked at me like I'd gone mad.

"I'm serious—it's stupid to think you can go around and practice self-will if you're going out of your mind with hunger. Why don't you try to give it another go? I can start by pushing my energy out. That might help?"

"Are you sure?" Hazel asked quietly. She must have been desperate.

"I'm sure," I promised.

"Thank you."

We turned to face one another, while Jenney stood at the other end of the table, watching. I focused on throwing my energy outward, hoping that Hazel would be intuitively apt enough to grasp hold of it. I felt the flickering sensation around my skull, and for a few moments I could feel Hazel latch onto my mind, slowly taking the energy that I was offering. Then, quickly, it became too much—the searing pain started again, and I gritted my teeth, trying not to call out.

"Stop!" Jenney yelled. "Hazel, try me."

The connection broke, and hastily I wiped away the tears of pain that had formed at the corners of my eyes. While the pain slowly ebbed away, Jenney went through the same experience, though she seemed to last longer than I did before grimacing and then crying out.

Jenney and I looked at each other, both pale and exhausted.

"I'm so sorry," Hazel whispered after a while. "I'm so, so sorry."

I shook my head, "Honestly, don't worry about it—it's fine."

"You are not fine!" Ash bellowed from the door of the kitchen, looking from me to Jenney. "What the *hell* has been going on?"

ASH

As soon as I entered the kitchen, I could sense something wasn't quite right with Ruby—it felt like all her energy had been nearly sucked dry, and she was as pale as a ghost. I looked at Jenney in disbelief. Surely she wouldn't have…

"Stop looking at me like that!" Jenney exclaimed, glaring back at me.

"Sorry," I retorted. "But what's going on, Ruby?"

She was looking up at me guiltily, and didn't say a word. I looked at Hazel for answers, but she had her head in her hands, avoiding looking at any of us. I heard Tejus striding in behind me.

"Hazel?" he asked, his voice full of concern. Tejus's complete one-eighty personality transformation around Hazel was taking some getting used to. It was so *weird* to hear him sounding caring and gentle toward someone. The only time I'd ever heard him adopt that tone in the past was with his bird.

"It's not going very well," Hazel muttered from behind her hands.

I'm missing something.

"Ruby? Will you please tell me what's going on?" I asked again.

"Why don't you ask Tejus?" she retorted, scowling at him. I looked at Tejus. The rest of us might as well not have existed—he was staring at Hazel like his world was falling apart, and even I could feel the tension radiating off his body.

I'm going to lose my temper.

"Will *someone* tell me what is going on?" I asked for the umpteenth time. Ruby sighed, nodding.

"You should sit down."

Ruby proceeded to tell me the story, and I sat awkwardly, not wanting to look at either Tejus or Hazel as their private life became public knowledge. Tejus paced up and down the kitchen the entire time, and I imagined he was blacking out our discussion as much as he could. When Ruby was finished, my only thought, other than concern for Hazel, was where in Nevertide that left Ruby and me.

I had never heard of anything like this happening. I still didn't understand *how* it could, but this wasn't the time or the place to ask questions. I would have to wait till I could speak to Tejus on his own. Maybe there was a way that it could be stopped, or reversed somehow.

Please let there be a loophole.

"We need to leave," Tejus announced coldly.

In that moment I pitied him. I might have envied Tejus all his life for his privileged upbringing, his confidence and self-assurance, and then his rise to king. But if he loved Hazel the way I loved Ruby, then he would never forgive himself for this.

"Where are you going?" Ruby asked.

"We're removing Jenus from his banishment," I said. "I need to beat him in another trial if I am to be named king."

"Are you kidding?" Ruby exploded. "That's insane!"

"After everything he's done?" Hazel asked Tejus, her expression horrified.

"There was nothing we could do," Tejus replied. "The only way the Impartial Ministers will accept Ash is if he is victorious over Jenus. The fools don't know what they're doing."

Hazel and Ruby were both silent for a few moments, no doubt reliving the nightmares that Jenus had put them through. Suddenly Hazel grinned.

"Well… at least I'll have someone to feed off of," she murmured. "I have no moral issues about syphoning as much as I want off *him*."

"Then let's get going. Hazel, you need to come. I don't think it's a good idea for you to be left alone," Tejus commanded, opening the door to the kitchen for us all to file out.

"Great," she muttered, "a road trip."

"If Hazel's going, then I'm going too."

Ruby jumped off her chair and walked toward the door. Tejus rolled his eyes, but didn't say anything. To be honest, I would be glad of the company—I wasn't exactly looking forward to a long ride with Tejus and Hazel being excruciatingly awkward with one another.

We left, Tejus taking one last look around the kitchen with an intrigued expression.

"You've never been down here before, have you?" I drawled.

"No. Can't say I have."

Right.

Of course not.

* * *

We had been traveling for miles. We passed through the forest, sticking to the open path, and then out into the meadows and grain crops where the borders of Hellswan stood.

"I remember this place," Ruby noted dryly, trotting alongside me on her bull-horse.

"Thought you might, Shortie."

A few miles ahead was where I'd dropped Ruby and her friends off, only to have them bouncing back a few moments later as the borders sprang them back into Hellswan. She winked at me, and I was glad that not all the memories of that day were bad ones for her. In my opinion, the first day I'd laid eyes on Ruby was one of the best of my life.

"Where are we going?" I called out to Tejus, who was riding upfront alongside Hazel.

"The forests that line the border, a little over to the left."

He pointed to a gloomy island of forestry in the distance, sprawling out from the smaller lines of trees that marked the end of the kingdom. Even in the afternoon sun, the place was surrounded by swirls of mist, making even the trees look gray.

"I wanted him further out, but we couldn't do it with the borders closed. Fortunate for us, I suppose." Tejus hit his heel against the flanks of the bull-horse and we all increased our pace, heading straight for the forest.

"Doesn't look very welcoming," Ruby noted with a shiver.

"Good," I retorted. "I hope the miserable bastard has hated every moment of it."

We slowed down as we reached the entrance. When I peered through the trees, the forest almost looked black— as dark and depressing a place as I'd ever seen. Even the earth seemed to smell dank and moldy, like there was nothing alive contained within it.

"We should dismount," Tejus informed us. "Guide the bullhorses in—the branches hang too low."

We all did as he asked, and a few moments later we were crossing the dead bracken and entering the oppressive gloom of the forest. I couldn't even hear the call of birds.

"What made you think of this place?" I asked Tejus, keeping my voice barely above a whisper.

"It has particular sentimental value to my brother," he replied.

"You put him somewhere he would like?" I asked, astonished.

Tejus grimaced.

"I didn't say he liked it."

Oh.

I marveled at more evidence of the Hellswan brotherly love. If I couldn't be responsible for the downfall of Queen Trina, I really hoped that it would be Tejus in charge of her punishment.

We carried on a bit further, Tejus leading with me bringing up the rear, until I could see the outline of a cave up ahead, a gaping black mouth and the curvature of the rock wild and overgrown with moss.

"Who goes there?" cried a voice barely recognizable as belonging to Jenus. He had always sounded reedy in comparison with his brothers, but now his tone was suffused with a cold, hollow fear.

"Your salvation, brother!" Tejus called back merrily. "At

the hands of those you harmed the most."

We stopped in front of the cave, but I couldn't hear anything other than the slow drip of water landing on stone, echoing from its depths. A second later, I heard the distinct sound of chains running across the earth, each link clanking as they unraveled. The sound was followed by heavy footsteps, moving slowly across stone, and the wheezing of an old man's breath.

Jenus stepped into the pool of light, standing just a little way back from the entrance to the cave. At first glance, I didn't recognize him. When I peered closer, I had the unmistakable feeling that whatever Jenus was on the inside was finally being shown on the outside. Gone was the slicked-back hair and icily aloof demeanor of Jenus the sentry prince. This creature was more beast than man. He was unshaven, with a filthy-looking beard that made the emaciation of his face all the more pronounced—the dark circles under his eyes made him look almost skeletal, and the shock of black hair that surrounded his skull made him look wild, deadly. His hands and feet were cuffed with iron bars, tied to a chain that led back into the cave.

"Have you come to mock?" Jenus spat. He eyed his brother as if none of the rest of us existed. "Handsome, honorable Tejus! The great, glorious Tejus! The monster with the concealed face! The swine, the bastard—the miserable child of a father who despised you and a mother who would sooner die than look at you! Have you, brother, come to offer me salvation?" The words ran like acid from his mouth—spittle flying, his face contorted with malevolence.

"Wow. Are we sure this is the best idea?" Ruby hissed at me. "He looks like a certifiable nutjob."

"Couldn't agree more." I grimaced.

"Hold your tongue, Jenus," Tejus replied in a bored voice. "The Impartial Ministers want you released. I'm looking forward to the moment they lay eyes on you." He smirked at his brother. "You look very kingly, I must say."

"Ah ha!" Jenus cried, practically foaming at the mouth. "Failed the Imperial trials already, fool brother? I have heard the trees whispering of your misdeeds…ice fires, rains of blood…it seems death follows you, Tejus. Oh, corrupted one!" He laughed madly for a few seconds, and then began to pace up and down, the chains sliding along in his wake.

"Wow," Hazel breathed.

"Ignore him." Tejus addressed us. "I need to remove the

boundary and then we'll tie him to one of the horses. Ruby, will you ride with Ash?"

"Of course," she agreed quietly. Her eyes hadn't left the mad mass of sentry flesh that was Jenus of Hellswan.

"Release me! Release me so that I might show you how it is done, brother! Hellswan should have always been mine—it was promised to *me*!"

Tejus rolled his eyes as he removed the borders and then stepped inside to gather up the chains. Jenus lunged for him as soon as he did, but Tejus was prepared, sidestepping his attack so that his brother fell forward and landed with a smack on the ground. Jenus lay there for a while, laughing.

Tejus gathered up the chains and then hauled him back up.

"Will you control yourself?" he hissed at his brother. "You are no more mad here than you were at home."

He dragged his brother over to Ruby's horse, and I pulled her away.

"Keep out of his way," I muttered. "He's obviously volatile."

"Yeah," she agreed, watching Tejus tie him to the horse. Jenus now had his gaze fixed on Hazel, smiling as she stood with her arms folded, glaring at him.

"I don't know why you're so angry." He smiled at her. "I let your brother live. He was nothing more than an amusing toy—a little puppet on strings...a little—"

"You do *not* get to mention my brother," Hazel growled at him.

"Or you'll do *what?*"

Tejus laughed out loud at his brother's challenge, and started tethering Jenus's horse to his own.

Jenus cried out in pain, collapsing forward on his bull-horse.

"STOP—please STOP!" he yelled, clutching at his head.

Tejus pulled on the reins of the bull-horse, and we started walking out of the forest. Jenus groaned, the pain of the syphoning carrying on.

"Brother," he cried, "stop—I beg you!"

"It's not Tejus, it's me," Hazel retorted, her pert nose wrinkling in satisfaction, "and this is payback."

Jenus whimpered once more, and then fell silent. When we reached the edge of the forest, Tejus looked back at his brother, laughing.

"Hazel, enough now. If you carry on he won't make it

back—he's weak enough as it is."

"Okay," she agreed, sighing.

A few moments later, Jenus started to stir. We were back riding through the cornfields now, not far from the storm cellar. Any pity I might have felt for Jenus was immediately erased. He had used all of them like playthings for his political gain, and as far as I was concerned, Jenus deserved everything that was coming his way.

Jenus started giggling again, and I let out a breath. Ruby rested her face against my back, turning it away from Jenus. I held her hands against my waist, idly rubbing my thumb against the smooth shells of her nails.

"Tejus, Tejus, what have you done?" Jenus laughed uproariously. Clearly he had lost all reason. If he had any sense he would keep his mouth well and truly shut. "Monster begat monster! How his lovely angel has fallen! My brother, the cancer that has corrupted beyond imagining…oh, how the mighty fall!"

"Ash, will you gag him?" Tejus muttered.

"Absolutely."

ROSE

I paced up and down the abandoned pub that we were using as our base. We were waiting for Mona to arrive with the other witches and GASP members. It would only take a few moments, but I still felt it was too long. I wanted to get back out there. I just couldn't accept the fact that the portal wasn't opening.

"They're here," Corrine announced, walking toward the door. Before she could reach it, Mona stepped inside, followed by the coven and Ashley and Landis, then Claudia and Yuri.

"I'm glad you found it," Mona said, greeting Corrine

and then glancing around at the rest of us. "We could have been out at sea for months."

"But it's shut," I replied, unable to look on the bright side at that moment.

"I know," Mona agreed, "but Rose, don't lose hope. Portals are there for one reason only—to give access to the supernatural dimension. Which means that if one exists, there's a way to get it open, no matter how hard it may seem."

I nodded. She was right, I supposed. I was losing perspective on this, and I couldn't afford to let my emotions get in the way. I *had* to stay clear-headed if we were going to have a chance at finding the kids.

"What do you suggest?" Corrine asked.

"Well, I need to see it first, but usually we would need someone on the other side of the portal willing to break it, which is obviously going to be tricky if we don't know where it leads or what species of supernatural resides within it."

"So we won't have enough power from just our side to break it?" I asked.

"I can't say that for sure, but it seems doubtful if Corrine has already tried with no results. However, if we

94

can get enough power on this side of the portal to work against it, we may find a way to break through."

I looked around at the ten witches gathered, not including Mona and Corrine. How much more power than this would we possibly need?

"Perhaps witches aren't our only answer," Corrine mused. "What about asking the jinn to help as well?"

"That could work," Mona agreed.

"Let me call my mom," I interjected.

"Good idea."

I picked up the phone and walked outside the pub. It was starting to rain, a gray sleet that was turning the sea more violent by the second.

"Mom?" I called out over the noise of the crashing waves. "Can you hear me?"

"Rose! Did you find anything?" Her voice came clearly through the line.

"We found a portal in the sea. We think it leads to the kids, but we can't open it—it's locked, or something. I've got Corrine and Mona here, but they think we need the help of a few jinn. Could you speak to Nuriya or Aisha? Their powers might be of help."

"Of course," she said. "I'm so glad you found something

at least. I'll get some jinn over right away—where am I sending them?"

"The Fair Isle off mainland Scotland…which is not very fair," I remarked, eyeing the run-down pub.

"Okay, I'll message you when they're on their way."

"Any news on Sherus's omen?" I asked before she hung up.

"Absolutely nothing. We're keeping our eyes open, but there's nothing so far. Your father is becoming agitated—he worries that we're in the eye of the storm, but neither of us can find anything that indicates something's wrong…though I suppose that probably means we're missing something."

"Okay, well… I'll talk to you later."

We hung up, and I made my way back inside. Claudia was arguing with Corinne about going to visit the portal before the jinn arrived, but Corinne wasn't having any of it.

"There's no point, Claudia. Better that we wait and then have a concentrated dose of power to try to break the portal. It will be no use if we tire ourselves before the jinn get here."

Claudia stormed off toward the bathrooms, and I

smiled weakly at Corrine, who rolled her eyes. This situation wasn't exactly bringing out the best in us, and Claudia was fiery on a normal day. But I understood her frustration.

"You okay?" Caleb asked, coming to stand next to me.

"I spoke to Mom. She's going to message me when the jinn are on their way. All we have to do is wait—"

A buzz emanated from my phone. Good, Mom worked fast. It was a message from her saying that Nuriya, Aisha and Horatio were coming. I sighed with relief and put the phone away.

"They're coming," I announced to everyone in the room. Turning back to Caleb, I rested my head on his shoulder. "I just want them home. I want to wake up in our house, and get the kids breakfast, and yell at Benedict to get started on his homework, and tell Hazel to put her e-reader down while she's at the dinner table."

Caleb pressed his lips to my forehead. "I know."

"How can we help?" Nuriya's voice interrupted my daydreaming. Looking over toward the bar, I saw that the jinn had arrived.

"Thank you for coming," Mona said to the jinn. "We need your help opening a portal—we think it's locked or stuck."

"Where?" Aisha asked, hands on her hips while her amethyst-colored eyes gazed around the pub. Her curly jet-black hair was swept above her head in a severe bun— it was her signature hairstyle for missions and made her look like she meant business.

"Out there," Corrine replied, pointing to the raging sea that could be seen from the windows.

Aisha's face scrunched in a grimace on taking in the view, before she straightened and announced, "Well, what are we waiting for? Let's go!"

Ruby

We approached a stone pavilion surrounded by forests on either side. The pavilion itself was crumbling and rotten—it had probably once been beautiful, but that had been a long time ago. Sentries milled about, all in their black cloaks and muttering and whispering among themselves. I squared my shoulders, wanting to face them with confidence.

The ride back to Hellswan with Jenus had been harrowing. Once we'd reached the gates, guards had come and removed him from our sight, probably to get him cleaned up before being presented to the rest of the royalty and the ministers. We'd had time to have baths, but before long we were back in the cold, hurtling through the air on vultures as I clung on to Ash's waist for dear life.

I wondered if Jenus had arrived yet, and I quickly scanned the crowd to see if I could locate him, but at this distance it was difficult to distinguish one sentry from the other.

Tejus and Ash led the way, with Hazel and I following behind. I hadn't really had a chance to talk to Ash, but I knew from the way he was marching ahead with Tejus, his back straight and his legs stiff, that he was probably on edge.

"Are you okay?" I asked Hazel quietly, before we reached the pavilion. She had been quiet on the ride back to the castle once she'd finished syphoning off Jenus, and then ridden on a vulture by herself, with Tejus controlling the bird with his mind.

"I'm okay... just trying not to be hungry," she murmured. "At least there are plenty of ministers here I don't like..."

I laughed out loud, and Tejus spun around.

"They're not going to like you being here"—he glared at us both—"so try to conduct yourselves in an orderly manner."

When he turned back around, Hazel rolled her eyes. It felt like we were naughty schoolchildren or something, being told off by our teacher.

"Don't mind him," Hazel whispered. "I think he's taking this worse than I am…"

I eyed her speculatively. "You do seem to be managing okay…are you sure you're not in denial or something?"

"I'm just trying not to think about it too much."

Right.

I didn't have the heart to tell her that was the very definition of denial. But before I could say another word, we'd reached the pavilion. Three ministers—seriously *old* ministers—were walking toward us, scowling.

"Explain this, Tejus!" one of them barked. "Humans!"

"Technically one human and a sentry," Tejus corrected him.

"What?"

"Nothing," he replied. "Minister, this trial is a kingship trial; the old rules should still apply. Kingship trials have always allowed spectators."

"I'm well aware of the rules, Tejus! But this is preposterous. We do not allow humans at the Pavilion.

This place is *sacred*."

I took another look at the place.

Really?

"I really didn't think it would be a problem," Tejus continued smoothly. "Ash brought along his chosen human, as he was permitted to do so in the kingship trials. Why would this be any different?"

The old minister glared at him, and then his eyes roved over to Hazel.

"And her? Is she for Jenus?"

In a split second, Tejus was face to face with the minister, his jaw clenched tightly.

"No," he bit out.

The minister stumbled back, and quickly righted himself.

"Very well. I'm sure there will be others willing to assist your brother." He cleared his throat, trying to regain his composure. Tejus relaxed slightly, stepping back.

"What is going on?" a familiar voice trilled from the crowd of ministers, and I saw the distinct royal-blue robes of Queen Trina. My entire body flushed with rage, and it took all my effort to stay standing and not run over to her and try to gouge out her eyes.

The minister looked at Tejus and then back at Queen Trina.

"The matter is settled," the minister mumbled. "Ash will have a human to syphon off, but only if Jenus is provided the same privilege."

Queen Trina smiled her sickly smile, directed at Tejus. Before she opened her mouth, I knew what she was going to do.

"Well, of course," she simpered, "I am a great supporter of those from royal bloodlines—I'd be happy to allow Jenus the privilege of syphoning off me."

You've changed your tune.

It wasn't long ago that Queen Trina had been a huge supporter of Ash, and firmly against Tejus. Clearly her plans, or more likely her *plot*, had changed.

"Though," she continued, "I don't know how fair that will be…Ash, your human looks a little pale. Have you not been getting out much?" She smiled at me for the benefit of the minster.

"I'm sure I'll be fine, but thank you so much for your concern," I replied without missing a beat. "I'm sure my youth and your *extensive* experience are equally matched."

Queen Trina's eyes flashed with rage as she held her

placid smile in place. She didn't reply, and I continued to grin at her. One day I would get my revenge on Queen Trina—perhaps not today, but that day would come.

Lithan hurried over, with Qentos behind him.

"Jenus of Hellswan is ready," Lithan declared.

I looked over to the pavilion. In the center I saw Jenus, his hair cut, his beard gone and wearing fresh robes. His feet and hands were now unbound, and he walked slowly around the circumference of the pavilion, muttering to himself. He might have been clean-shaven, but he looked just as crazy as when I'd seen him last.

We made our way up the stone steps, and I took the opportunity to grab hold of Ash's hand and squeeze it tightly. I wanted him to know that I supported him, that I believed he could do this. His fingers closed around mine briefly and then released me.

"Sentries, kings," another of the ancient-looking ministers announced, "as Tejus has forfeited his crown, the Imperial trials will continue once a new Hellswan champion is chosen."

The crowd didn't make a sound. The only noise that could be heard was the scratching of some stray leaves scuttling along the stone ground.

"Each contender will be provided with a sword, and they will battle one another using the weapon *only*. Jenus will syphon-pair with Queen Trina Seraq, and Ashbik will syphon-pair with a human."

"*Ruby*," Ash interrupted.

"Yes, Ruby." The minister glared at him, but then continued. "The battle is won when one of you surrenders or concedes. May the best sentry win."

The ministers and the other royals stood back. Only one of the old ministers remained, handing swords to Ash and Jenus.

My heart leapt into my throat. I watched as Ash took the sword, thanking the minister with a small bow. When it came to Jenus, he snatched the sword from the minister and held it aloft, his hands and arms shaking in anticipation. He looked like a crazed, rabid beast, foam and spittle forming at the edge of his mouth as he prepared to take Ash down.

"Kitchen boy, see this sword?" he sneered. "It will be as close as you ever get to royalty when your blood wets its tip!"

Ash didn't reply; he just watched Jenus, taking in the shaking arms, the bulging eyes and the thin, malnourished frame.

You can do this, Ash.

I hoped he could hear me. I was waiting impatiently for him to syphon off me, trying to keep my mind as focused as possible for when he needed it. But I also knew from experience that Ash preferred to play the more strategic long game. He would wait till he really needed me before taking my energy.

The pair circled one another, moving slowly. I could hear both of their breaths—Ash's even and controlled, Jenus's rasping and excited. I looked over at Queen Trina. She was keeping the smug smile on her face, but leaning against one of the arches with perspiration lightly smattering her forehead. Jenus must be syphoning off her. I knew from experience just how painful that could be.

Good.

I hoped it hurt like hell.

Suddenly Jenus lunged, sword pointed toward Ash's chest. I suppressed a cry as Ash dodged the blade and shifted into position behind Jenus to strike back. Jenus's sword crashed against his, and both weapons clanged with a deafening screech of steel on steel. Jenus's attacks were wild and unrestrained. He spun around madly, cloak flying and screaming bizarre obscenities. Ash was far more measured, each attack more calculated and aimed. In any other fight it would have benefited him, his aim almost always perfect. But this fight wasn't like any other—against the animalistic rage of Jenus, Ash was starting to tire.

Please—please, Ash, take my energy!

I called to him mentally, pleading to have him use me. Queen Trina was fading. Her face had turned a pasty, wax-like color and I knew that now was Ash's best chance of gaining the upper hand.

Ash! I cried, throwing out my energy.

Finally, he reciprocated and I could feel the tingling sensation of his syphon spreading across my mind. It made me feel warm and fuzzy for a while, until I could feel the more urgent tug of Ash consuming all that I had to offer. It was making me unsteady on my feet, but it was working.

Ash's lunges were coming harder and faster. Jenus was starting to look panicked. A second later, Ash landed a blow on Jenus's upper arm. Blood sprayed onto the stone floor and then started to soak his gown. I hoped the blow would make Jenus nervous, but it seemed to do the opposite. His attacks became even more ferocious, his spittle and blood flying about as he launched himself at Ash again and again. This time Ash was better prepared—he blocked the wild slashes of Jenus's sword, gaining ground as he moved slowly toward him. Jenus threw his weight behind one final aim. When Ash blocked it, sliding Jenus's sword off the blade of his own, Jenus fell backward onto the floor of the pavilion.

Ash placed the tip of his blade on Jenus's jugular.

"Do... you...surrender?" he panted.

Jenus growled at him from the ground, causing Ash to put more pressure on his blade.

Jenus let his head fall back onto the stone.

"I surrender," he whispered. "I surrender."

I felt my whole body go weak with relief. Ash had done it.

Ash dropped the sword to the floor with a clatter, and I rushed forward, not caring how inappropriate it might have seemed to the watching sentries.

"You did it!" I breathed, as Ash picked me up in one swift movement and gathered me up into his arms.

"Thanks, Shortie," he murmured against me. "Once again, I couldn't have done it without you."

I didn't want to let go.

I heard the sounds of polite clapping from some of the ministers, and Memenion shouted out a sincere congratulations, but other than that, the pavilion had fallen silent once again. This was a wildly different atmosphere from the original kingship trials.

"I should get off you, shouldn't I?" I whispered in Ash's ear.

His low laugh rumbled against me.

"Probably," he replied, and I could feel him smiling.

I dropped down, and looked for Tejus and Hazel. They were standing a few feet apart, and Hazel was beaming broadly, mouthing a 'congratulations'. Tejus was smiling, but it didn't meet his eyes. It must have been painful for him to witness, to know that Ash had just become king of Hellswan. Tejus's birthright—his home. Hazel followed my gaze, and as she looked at Tejus her face softened. She gave him a reassuring smile, but I noticed that she didn't dare touch him...

Oh.

You idiot.

I'd spent all day worrying about Hazel and her future, and then the trials, that I'd completely failed to notice the massive, huge, horrifying pink elephant in the room.

Oh, my God.

If Hazel had become a sentry because she was intimate with Tejus…then where did that leave me and Ash?

My face must have gone white, because Hazel rushed up to me, her eyes full of concern. "Ruby, what's up? Are you okay?" she asked.

"Yeah…I'm fine," I replied slowly. "I just…realized something. But it's nothing," I amended. "I think I left something at the castle."

"What?" asked Hazel, looking at me oddly.

"Um, my…lucky penny."

"Your lucky penny?" Hazel repeated.

"Yep."

"Okay. I didn't realize you had a lucky penny. Clearly you didn't need it?" she questioned, talking to me like I was a small child.

"No. Obviously not."

"Right. Okay, you need some sleep," she asserted, clearly thinking that I was starting to go mad. The annoying thing was I *wanted* to talk to her about it— desperately—but this just wasn't the right place or time…and it would probably be more sensible to talk to Ash about it first.

I felt my body go cold with dread. Were we never going to be able to be…close to one another? The thought was horrible. I really wanted to be with Ash, in every way. But if I had to make the choice…

Stop.

There was no point making imaginary decisions about it until I knew for sure. There might well be a way to stop that from happening. Someone would *have* to know a way, surely?

"Congratulations, Ashbik!" One of the ministers stepped forward. His cry was booming, but I could tell by his dead, black, shark eyes that he didn't mean it. No one here, other than Memenion or Tejus, wanted Ash to be king. Let alone emperor.

"The coronation will begin tomorrow morning," the minister continued, "and then the trials will re-commence."

King Ash of Hellswan.

I wasn't actually sure if I liked the sound of that.

JENUS

Defeated by a kitchen boy.

I had never suffered such shame in all my life. And with my brother watching, his lips twitching into a smile as the boy degraded me. I should never have had to battle him—that crown belonged to me! It was mine by right. My father had wanted *me* to wear it; the kingdom had been promised to me—I had always been the favored son in his eyes.

Now I was ruler of nothing. A dank cave, if I wished it, but I had no other home to go to. I'd had one chance to regain power, and I had single-handedly destroyed it. But no wonder! I had been half-starved, unable to syphon off anything other than small rodents that made the mistake of scurrying into my path. All the other creatures had stayed well away.

I was still lying on the cold stone of the pavilion floor. Warm blood still seeped into my robes.

Dusk was here, the shadows of the surrounding forests creeping up over me. I had half expected guards to seize me and return me to my hell hole, but none had arrived yet – I could see them up ahead in the distance, no doubt discussing what should be done with me. Tejus and the kitchen king had already left...I supposed they no longer considered me to be a danger... too weak to pose a threat.

They would be proved wrong.

"Jenus, you look uncomfortable."

A treacle-like voice oozed from the darkness. Queen Trina approached the steps up to the pavilion, her beautiful face half-cast in darkness.

"Mind your own business!" I hissed, spitting a globule of phlegm in her direction.

She merely smiled, side-stepping the spittle.

"Charming," she retorted.

I sighed, resting my head back on the stone.

She-devil.

I loathed Queen Trina. I wasn't alone in that, I was sure. As a young boy, I had loved her, fascinated with her dark, thick hair and her almond eyes, and the soft mocking of her smile. I had worshiped her from afar, waiting for my moment, waiting till I was man enough to woo her. I had been a fool. With the same reverence I held for her, she'd attached herself to Tejus, plotting and scheming her way into his life—on occasion using me as a pawn just to get close to him. To make him love her. My handsome, arrogant brother, the monster who had everything, and hated himself for it.

"Go away," I sighed. "I don't want or need your help."

"It doesn't look that way," she remarked, as casually as if we were two people having a picnic in a park.

"What do you want?" I asked, changing tactics. I was too tired and humiliated to play games.

"To help you," she replied simply.

"And what scheme would that play into? Is it another arrow to be aimed at Tejus's heart? I have news for you— he has evidently moved on." I smiled to myself. I knew *that* comment would enrage her.

She was silent for a few moments.

"I know how you feel," she whispered eventually. "I know what humiliation is. I know what it's like to be shut out in the cold by Tejus. I know what a desperate place that is. I've been there."

"I do *not* care what Tejus thinks of me," I snapped back.

"Perhaps not," she conceded, "but where else are you going to go? You are an enemy of Hellswan now, Jenus. Perhaps you might join me instead. You and I are survivors—the ones who stand back and witness the rise of others, and then their eventual downfall, all the while maintaining our balance."

"You don't think *this* is a downfall?" I raged.

She shrugged. "You are alive. You are in a better position than you think, Jenus."

"How so?"

"There is a dark power coming. An ancient one, once king of all, cut down by the very men who served him. Once he is risen, he will restore true balance. Come to my kingdom—help me. Share in my glory, Jenus."

Queen Trina's words sounded utterly implausible, and yet they sent a shiver of fear running down my spine. I had never heard her talk with such seriousness, such awe. Did she really believe that an ancient power was rising? *What* power? *What* glory?

"You're making no sense," I replied curtly.

"Oh, but I will if you come with me."

"Why, if you're so eager for me to join you, did you not rescue me from that abysmal cave?"

At this, Queen Trina laughed. "Where would the fun have been in that?" she asked. "Jenus, all things happen in their own time. Events thus far have been just as they should be. Surprising, yes, but eventually satisfactory. Join me, Jenus," she said again. "You will not regret it."

I assessed my options—it didn't take long.

It was either the cave or the Seraq kingdom, known for its lavish opulence and comfort. I would be a fool to turn her down…and even if it meant I was willingly becoming a pawn in whatever political game she was playing, at least I would be a well-fed and warm one.

"Agreed," I sighed, sitting up.

Queen Trina smiled in the darkness, her eyes almost luminous as she fixed her gaze on me. Suddenly, I felt more like prey than political pawn.

SHERUS

I was escorted through The Shade with two of my guards, led by yet another witch to the treehouse apartments where Ben and Derek lived with their families. They were curious places—modern, from what I understood of the human world, and beautifully constructed, but I had no real idea as to why they lived among the trees and were not content with the ground.

When we reached the door, the witch knocked, clearing her throat as if she was nervous about approaching the inhabitants. She was young—I imagined she was some kind of novice, a younger generation of a coven that hadn't yet reached the height of her powers.

Derek opened the door, smiling politely when he saw me, but eyeing my guards with suspicion.

"Thank you, Arwen." He nodded at the witch. "You can leave us."

She nodded back, and without another word she turned and left, disappearing down beneath the wooden veranda.

"I see you have brought company," he observed, regarding my armed companions with interest.

"Telis and Kelit. They are my most trusted guards—I hoped they could help us."

Derek nodded, standing aside to let us inside.

"You're all welcome."

We followed Derek into the living room, where Benjamin stood waiting.

"Sherus." He nodded in greeting. "Do you have news?"

"I have persuaded the fae to unite. All the kingdoms will now work together when the threat shows itself. It is the first time in many, many years that a treaty of this kind has been reached. Long may it continue."

Benjamin listened to what I had to say, but I noticed his glance often returning to the guards behind me. His expression was curious, and I could see that the boy still had questions about the nature of the body he inhabited.

"Unfortunately, we haven't been able to unearth anything yet," Derek replied.

I had expected this. The more I thought about it, the more I was convinced that whatever was rising would somehow be under the radar of all of us, potentially undetected before it was too late. It would explain why the omens presented to me were so strong; the stars always had a way of compensating for the frailty of the mortal.

"Which is why we have come to assist you," I replied. "I believe that the threat is going to come from your world, not ours."

"What makes you say that?" Benjamin asked.

"I feel it," I replied. "And the stars do not lie."

Benjamin nodded, but I could sense his skepticism. It didn't bother me—he still had a lot to learn about our kind, and the connection that all fae had to nature, quite different to all other supernatural creatures.

"Then we welcome you here," Derek announced. "There are mountain cabins where you can stay, which I hope you'll find to your liking."

"Thank you," I replied, grateful that I wouldn't be living in these strange tree contraptions, as elegant as they were.

A few moments later I bid Derek goodbye while Benjamin led us to the cabins where we would be staying. After a few more curious glances at my guards, he left us to make ourselves at home, asking us to reconvene in an hour to go over all the research they'd unearthed so far.

Telis and Kelit positioned themselves outside of my front door. They would not rest while I was here, untrusting of the strange land they found themselves in, and wary of its inhabitants.

I bathed to refresh myself, and when I'd finished, a knock came from the door. I hastened to answer it—the hour had not yet passed, and I hoped this meant that Derek might have some news. As soon as I saw his face, it was clear that he did not.

"What is it?" I asked, noting his bemused expression.

Before he could reply, my flame-haired sister stepped into view.

"Did you think you could leave me out of all this, Sherus?" she demanded.

"Lidera." I sighed. "What is the meaning of this?"

"I'm here to stop you from making any ridiculous mistakes—and to keep you company."

"So you might abandon me at the final hour?" I asked sarcastically, recalling the time she had left me in The Underworld.

"Sherus," she warned, "stop bringing up ancient history and let me help you."

There would be no use arguing with her. When Lidera made up her mind, that was usually the end of it.

"Can The Shade accommodate one more fae?" I asked King Derek politely.

"Of course," he replied. "We will see to it."

I let Lidera enter the cabin, and groaned inwardly.

HAZEL

When we arrived back at the castle, I headed straight for Tejus's living quarters. I wanted to join in the celebrations with Ash and Ruby, but as the servants and the kids gathered around to admire the soon-to-be-king Ash, I felt overwhelmed by my hunger – the constant repression of it was making me tired and irritable.

I tried to slip away unnoticed, but as soon as I entered the living room, Tejus appeared in the doorway – remaining at the entrance to give me some space.

"How are you?" he asked, arms folded across his chest as he leaned against the frame.

"I'm… okay. I was getting a headache being around all those people…the hunger gets worse the more tired I get."

He nodded in understanding. "You should get some rest. You won't be able to fight it off if you're sleep-deprived. Trust me."

I raised my eyebrows at Tejus's admission. *When has he not been able to hold back?*

He smiled. "It can get quite bad during sentry teenage years, let's leave it at that."

Hormones out of control … I guessed that would make an extra impact. Certainly, whenever Tejus was around I felt the hunger and all the crazy emotions that went with it peak and dive like a rollercoaster. Not that, when it came to him, I was much different when I was human…

"Can I come in?" he asked.

I frowned. "Uh, yes. It's your home."

"I'm trying to give you space. I don't want to make this any harder for you."

"You're not," I lied. I wanted him around – it wasn't only the hunger that drew me to him, after spending the night together I couldn't stop thinking about the way his skin had felt brushing against mine, his kisses that had run all over my body, the silent exhales that had escaped his lips and mine…Being near him, but not able to touch him, was driving me crazy. Like I didn't have *enough* crazy to deal with.

"I'm going to take a bath anyway," I announced. I desperately needed something comforting and warm – if it wasn't going to be Tejus's embrace, then a bath would have to do.

"I'll meet you here when you're done."

"Okay," I gulped. There was something about the way he'd worded that statement which made my legs feel weak and the pit of my stomach knot.

I made my way to the bathroom, and after running the faucet for a while, I stepped into the near-boiling water – fragrantly scented with oils and dried petals. I leaned my head against the edge of the tub, feeling the tension in my muscles finally relax…

I woke up to cold water and Lucifer meowing outside the door. I must have drifted off. Hastily, I wrapped a towel around me and went back to the living room. Tejus had lit a fire, and was sitting on one of the velvet sofas idly flicking through one of the ministers' volumes.

"You were gone a while," he observed, his dark eyes

lazily wandering up and down my body.

"I fell asleep, sorry."

I felt hugely self-conscious standing in the living room with just a towel on, and without waiting for him to say another word, I slipped into the spare room to put on some clothes. I heard Tejus rise from the sofa.

"I would like it if you would sleep in my room tonight," he spoke.

I paused briefly before quickly wrapping myself in a robe.

"But...we can't..." I trailed off.

"I know," he replied, appearing before me. "But it's where you belong – still. Even if I can't hold you."

I thought about the request, heat rising in my cheeks when I thought of the bed – in my mind I would forever remember it covered with tangled sheets, and Tejus leaning up against the headboard.

"Okay," I breathed.

He stepped back out of the spare room, clearing his throat.

"I'll let you get comfortable," he said, gesturing toward his bedroom.

Unable to look him in the eye, I hastened to the room.

My stomach was fluttering wildly, and I noticed the complete absence of my hunger – replaced by surging emotions and feelings of a totally different kind.

The bed had been re-made. I walked over to the frame, sliding beneath the cool sheets with my head propped up against the pillows. I started to notice things I hadn't before – the way the decoration in this room was slightly different to the rest of the living quarters. It was more sparse – the crushed red velvet replaced by dark wools and oak. It suited Tejus more than the other rooms.

"Where are you going to sleep?" I asked Tejus as he made his way into the room, carrying a coverlet and a cushion.

"On the floor," he replied.

"Oh."

I had thought that he would be sleeping in the spare room or on one of the sofas – surely that would be more comfortable?

"Problem?" he asked wryly.

"No...won't you be uncomfortable?"

He shrugged. "No. I don't see why I would."

"I feel guilty," I burst out. "I should sleep back in the –

"

"No," Tejus interjected. "Please Hazel. I feel bad enough having been intimate with you without us being married – it is not the sentry culture, and definitely not the accepted behavior of a royal. The only reason I didn't ask you to wed me was because of the ceremony – I wasn't willing to risk it...more of my foolishness. However, I am certainly not willing to go on as we were before – you're mine, and I intend for it to stay that way – no matter how difficult our path together may be."

Wow.

Marriage?

I didn't realize Tejus felt that way...I was speechless; completely thrown by his honesty. I felt the heat rising once again in my cheeks.

"Do you not feel the same way?" he asked.

"I do," I whispered. "I just didn't know..."

"Now you do," he replied. His eyes grew hooded and dark, watching me from the foot of the bed. Every bone in my body, every single particle that made me who and what I was, screamed out to touch him – to feel the hard, sinewy muscle of him under my hands, and his firm lips pressed against mine. Now that I knew what sensations and emotions Tejus could bring up in me, I would never get enough of him…I would never want to be apart from him.

He smiled softly, his eyes changing from lustful to gentle in a moment. He carelessly threw the bedding onto the floor, and then removed his robe and shirt – flinging those on an armchair in the corner of the room. I held my breath, my mouth running dry as I observed his scar-torn, muscled chest.

"I will ask you properly, Hazel. When the time is right…I mean it. I want you to be mine, always."

I nodded, swallowing. "Always," I whispered.

Between Tejus and me, I could no longer imagine it being any other way.

HAZEL

I didn't sleep well.

I spent the night hyper-aware of Tejus sleeping so close to me, my body tossing and turning as I grew too hot and then too cold – frustration burning through my nerves; wishing throughout the night that he would join me…and then running over and over his request that we be married someday. I had tried to think about it logically – to understand if I was ready for such a huge commitment…but I swiftly became distracted by the overwhelming feelings I had for him – where logic just didn't come into it.

When I did sleep, I had horrible dreams where I thought Benedict was syphoning off someone, only to realize that it was me doing the syphoning…

It was now the morning of Ash's coronation and I was back in the spare room getting dressed in the only attire I had that was suitable—the dress I'd worn to Tejus's coronation. The dress that I'd been wearing when Tejus had first kissed me.

This time I was spared the awkwardness of having servants dress me, though it made some of the job problematic as I couldn't do up the back on my own. I heard Tejus pacing impatiently outside my room. I sighed.

Behold the awesome power of a sentry. I can't even dress myself.

I opened the door, and came face-to-face with Tejus. He was wearing black robes, his long hair pulled back in the leather tie and his face freshly shaven. I'd prepared myself for feeling the pang of mental hunger when I saw him this morning—but not the electric shocks of lust and want that coursed through my body. His dark eyes latched onto mine, his pupils dilating.

"Hi," I murmured. "I need help with my dress."

"Right," he replied, his voice hoarse.

I turned around, moving my hair to the side. A moment later his fingers brushed against my spine, carefully buttoning the million pebble-sized beads that held the dress together. I felt goosebumps rise up all over my body in response.

"Sorry, my hands are cold."

"It's fine." I swallowed. "It's an annoying dress."

"It's a beautiful dress," he replied softly, hooking the final button. Carefully he reached for my hair, letting it cascade back down.

"Thank you."

"You're welcome."

He must have moved his head closer toward me, as the next moment I could feel his warm breath on my hair—but I could also sense his mind…and it sent a wave of hunger washing over me, obliterating the more carnal desire I'd felt only seconds before.

I stepped hastily away.

"I'm worried and relieved that Benedict didn't come back last night," I babbled. "Did you see or hear anything?"

"He may have returned," Tejus replied, "but I wouldn't be the first to know. Ash would."

Oh. Right.

"Okay. I guess we'll speak to him after the coronation."

Tejus nodded.

I looked back up at him, trying to read his expression. I wondered how he felt, having Ash take his place. I imagined that he would see it as a lack of control—and for Tejus of all people, I imagined that would be difficult to take.

"Do you have to attend the coronation?" I asked softly.

He smiled and rose his eyebrow.

"Yes, Hazel, I have to attend the coronation. Do you think I'm going to fall apart because I've lost my beloved kingdom?" he asked dryly.

I rolled my eyes. How could he not take this seriously?

"Obviously not," I retorted. "But I did think you might be a bit upset...or, I don't know, have some kind of emotion going on behind that mask?"

"I do have an emotion going on," he replied.

"And?"

He exhaled. "It's frustration. I am frustrated that I can't kiss you, or touch you, or be near you without you wanting to feed off my energy."

"You've lost your kingdom, and that's all you can think

about?" I asked, trying not to let my reaction to his words show. Perhaps I had been living in denial. His frustrations were mine too, and all I wanted to do was get swallowed up in his arms again.

"That's all I can think about, yes."

"I'm flattered," I replied, teasingly. "Who knew you were such a romantic?"

He snorted with derision, folding his arms across his chest.

"Hardly."

"I know one when I see one, trust me."

I thought of my addiction to romance e-books…or my past addiction. Obviously, I hadn't been able to get hold of one here, but the girl who liked nothing more than to curl up on a sofa with a romance seemed so far removed from who I was now. Like we were a million light years away from one another. I guessed that along the way, the dimensions which separated my normal life from this one had started to become more than just geography.

"Are you still here?" Tejus asked, smirking at me.

"Sorry." I blushed. "I was just thinking…so much has changed. It's weird."

"It doesn't have to be 'weird' forever. Later we're going

to practice syphoning—and we'll continue to do it until you get your hunger under control. You'll be able to live an ordinary life. I promise."

I nodded, not really knowing if I was capable of having an ordinary life. Whatever that was.

"I really don't want to hurt you," I objected. "Can't I practice on Lithan or someone equally mean and pointless?"

Tejus laughed out loud.

"We could try, but trust me, you'll have a far more pleasant experience with me."

I believe that.

"I also need to see my brother," I reminded him. "It's been too long since I spoke to him properly."

Tejus nodded. "I thought about that—it may be worth doing as the sun sets. If we stay there, we might be able to see what happens... where he takes the stones, what he does with them, if anyone joins him. There's still so much we don't know."

"Good plan. But let's get there a bit earlier than sunset—I want to be able to speak to him before...you know, he *changes*."

"All right... Are you ready?" he asked.

"Yes." I took one last look at my dress, smoothing out the flow of the material. I hoped I wasn't overdressed.

"You look incredible," Tejus murmured as he opened the door.

Despite the lack of official announcement and celebration at the actual trial, word had clearly gotten around. The hallway was buzzing with villagers, kids running about the place and men cheering for their hero—Ash.

Tejus stalked through the crowds, and I hurried to stay by his side. The villagers parted as we approached, falling silent as their old king passed. I cursed my sentry affliction, not for the first time. I wanted to comfort Tejus more than I could bear—even just a brush of my hand against his to know he wasn't alone.

When we entered the coronation room, it was packed. The obligatory ministers stood at the front, a mass of black robes and solemn faces. The villagers had crowded in at the back, jostling for the best vantage point. It was crowded, and I started to panic. With this many minds gathered in one room, I didn't know if I was going to be able to control myself.

"Hazel, follow me, hold on to my robe if you need to," Tejus commanded.

Like in the hallway, the crowds parted when they saw him coming and I was given a bit of breathing space as we made our way to stand against the left-hand wall of the room.

I leaned against the stone wall with Tejus next to me. Here we had a good view of the throne that Ash would be seated in. There was no second chair, and I wondered if Tejus had insisted on it during his coronation. I scanned the room for Ruby, but I couldn't see her—she was probably waiting with Ash.

The minister of ceremonies, whom I recognized from the trials, stood up on the dais.

"Sentries! Please be seated for your king, Ashbik of Hellswan!"

The minister certainly sounded more positive calling out Ash's name than he had in the past—clearly he realized that there would be a lot of sucking up to do in order to redeem himself in the eyes of the new king. He wouldn't be the only one. Lithan and Qentos sat right at the front. Lithan's face was like thunder.

Ash entered to applause, and Ruby crept in from the

back of the room. She looked for a seat, but couldn't find any, so I gave her a small wave and she came to stand next to us.

"Quite a crowd, right?" Her blue eyes widened in surprise as she took in the full extent of the audience.

The minister droned on, going into great detail about the nature of a king's duty to his kingdom and its people. It was the same stuff that had been said at Tejus's coronation, and coming from the minister it sounded just as hollow and meaningless today as it did then.

"We're going to see Benedict before sunset today at the temple, and then wait around to see what happens when the sun goes down," I whispered, gritting my teeth against the tugs of hunger that were pulsing through me from being so close to Ruby.

"That sounds like a good plan." She nodded. "I'll see if Ash can come too."

I guessed I had to get used to Ash and Ruby being a package deal from now on. It wasn't that I didn't like Ash—I did, but after he had voluntarily decided to work with Queen Trina, I had my misgivings about his judgment…not that I could really talk. I was just watching out for Ruby, and I had no doubt that she probably thought that Tejus was an equally inappropriate match for me. She was just too good a friend to say anything.

I looked over at Tejus.

The words of the minister floated over. "...to pledge one's life to the protection and care of a kingdom and its people is a great honor. It should not be taken lightly, but with reverence and dedication, a determination to put others before oneself. To rule fairly, to rule bravely, to rule with heart as well as mind. To undertake the sacrifices that go with such a position, and to undertake them with grace and dignity. To be honest above all else—about your own limitations, and others'. To love your people as if they are your own children, to care, protect and love..."

Tejus might never realize it, but he had fulfilled his duty to his people in the short time he had ruled. The night that he had abdicated the throne was, ironically, the night that I had believed wholeheartedly he *was* made to rule and lead—and if it wasn't going to be at Hellswan, it would be somewhere else.

The crown was lowered on to Ash's head.

Tejus stood, perfectly erect and silent against the wall, his eyes fixed on the ceremony. My heart broke for him. He did care about losing the crown, but he would never show it because of all the attributes the minister had just listed. Bravery, dignity, honesty, determination. Tejus had all of those qualities in abundance—and although few people in this room knew it, Tejus had just selflessly lost everything in the hope that he might save Nevertide from the deadly clutches of Queen Trina.

ASH

It was over.

The ministers left the dais, and I searched the room for Ruby. She was standing over by Tejus and Hazel at one end of the room. Her gaze met mine through the crowd. She smiled at me, and it seemed genuine enough, but I noticed the lack of sparkle in her eyes. Ruby always smiled at me like she was contemplating her own private joke—that whatever the situation, she was finding humor in it somewhere. That was one of the things I loved about her; she was challenging. I could win every single one of the Imperial trials and it wouldn't make me feel as victorious as the moments when I managed to make Ruby laugh.

I stood stiffly up from the chair—it wasn't the most comfortable seat I'd ever sat on, and already the crown was starting to make my neck ache. It was also strange sitting in the seat that Tejus had occupied only a week ago. It didn't feel like it belonged to me. I felt like an imposter, playing the role of king while the real one stood, practically shunned by his subjects, a few yards away.

I'd glanced over at him a few times during the ceremony. He had kept his eyes fixed on the dais, and as the minister of ceremony had droned on, Tejus had remained motionless, as if he was genuinely listening to every word the sentry said. I hadn't been able to attend the actual ceremony of Tejus's crowning. I had felt too bitter and twisted up inside to watch. But he had braved mine, and once again I started to feel like perhaps Tejus was a better man than I had ever given him credit for.

I noticed that he and Hazel had stood a few feet apart throughout the ceremony. I still hadn't had a moment to ask Tejus about the logistics behind the transformation, or if there was any way of avoiding it. It wasn't a conversation I was looking forward to. There would be no way of phrasing it that wasn't going to be excruciatingly awkward for both of us.

But I had to know.

Because if there was only one conclusion, only one possible outcome, then both Ruby and I had some tough decisions to make.

I started down the small steps of the dais, smiling at the ministers who insincerely congratulated me. The villagers were being moved out of the hall as quickly as possible by the guards. I didn't like the implication that they weren't welcome.

Then I realized I could do something about it.

"Hey!" I called to one of the guards who was firmly, but not unkindly pushing a family out of the door, "Enough."

He spun around, and bowed when he saw who had interrupted him.

"I'm sorry, your highness, the ministers said that villagers should be escorted out."

"The ministers are wrong. I know there's food laid out for all the Hellswan subjects—the villagers will feast with them too. There's more than enough to go around."

"Yes, your highness." The guard nodded quickly.

"Thank you, your highness," intoned the father of the family. "We had high hopes for you, and it looks like we weren't wrong. Once one of us, always one of us, didn't I tell you?" He nudged his wife, who loosened her grip on her two children and beamed up at me.

"You did. Thank you, your highness. We're very grateful," she responded.

I nodded, feeling uncomfortable with my new title. It just didn't seem like it *belonged* to me, and I doubted that it ever really would.

"Ashbik!" a familiar voice cried out. That was more like it!

"Hello, Abelle." I smiled as she drew me into a slightly overpowering, floral-scented hug. Eventually she drew me back at arm's length, inspecting me.

"Every inch the king," she declared.

"It doesn't feel that way. I keep thinking someone's going to come and drag me back into the kitchens and stick me in an apron."

Abelle laughed.

"If that were the case, you'd still be a king, Ash. It's not in the title or in the clothing—it's what's inside of you. And you, my boy, were born to lead."

"Thanks." I nodded, feeling awkward but pleased. I knew that most of the ministers opposed my position—

they'd be waiting in the wings for me to do something wrong. Just knowing that I had supporters and sentries who believed in me helped. It reminded me why I'd wanted to do this all along. It wasn't for me, it was for *them*.

"I'm glad to see you survived the ice fires. Your shop's still standing?" I asked.

"It's all in one piece. Yes, the ice fires and the blood rain weren't exactly ideal, but I managed. Plenty didn't. A lot of livestock's gone—and most of the fields are ruined," she added, raising her eyebrows. "You're going to have a lot on your plate, Ashbik…"

"I know," I replied. "I'm ready."

She beamed at me again. "I know you are."

I was about to excuse myself when Ruby's hand brushed against my arm in greeting.

"Ruby!" Abelle exclaimed before I could speak. "It's good to see you again. Thank you for keeping Ashbik alive."

Ruby laughed. "Actually I think it was the other way around…but I'll take the praise anyway."

What are they talking about?

"Going to let me in on the joke?" I asked, bemused.

"Nope," Ruby replied, placing her hand around my arm in a sweet, familiar gesture. "Sorry."

Ruby turned back to Abelle, all traces of laughter gone.

"There was something I wanted to ask you about. It's for my friend, Hazel. She's recently become a...a *sentry*." She delivered the word with difficulty, gulping. "She doesn't have much control over her syphoning powers—I was wondering if you had anything that might help? Some herbs or something she could take?"

"A sentry?" Abelle questioned with disbelief. "My goodness..."

I could see Abelle's mind whirring as she contemplated what Ruby had just said.

"Well...that must mean that she married, err...who?" Abelle stuttered.

"Not *exactly*." Ruby blushed, "and it was Tejus."

Abelle looked confused for a moment, before comprehension dawned on her. "Oh!" she exclaimed. "I see."

There was a long pause. I could see Abelle trying her best not to appear too shocked, while Ruby squirmed and I prayed that Abelle would announce she had a cure to reverse the transformation.

"Well," Abelle replied eventually, "there are herbs…certain concoctions that I can create that should repress the more intense impulses to syphon—things that Hazel can take while she learns to get her powers under control—but the hard work she will need to do herself. She will need to put in practice and be patient while she masters the sentry abilities."

"But nothing that can reverse it?" I asked quietly.

"Nothing that I know of," Abelle replied. "I'm sorry."

It wasn't what I wanted to hear.

I looked over at Ruby, but her gaze was fixed on the floor.

"I'll leave you two," Abelle announced suddenly. "I've just spotted an old friend. Let Hazel know she's welcome to come over and visit any time—I'll help her in any way I can."

"Thanks, Abelle," Ruby replied. "I'll let her know."

"Good luck, Ashbik."

As soon as Abelle left us, a thick tension descended between Ruby and me. There were so many things I wanted to say to her, but I didn't even know where to begin. I didn't even know if Ruby was even thinking about *us*—maybe she was solely focused on her friend.

Please say something.

Neither of us spoke for a while. I kept smiling and nodding at villagers who waved and shouted in my direction, but my heart wasn't in it. I felt slightly sick, like the walls were crashing in slow motion around me—the idea of Ruby and me not being able to be together was starting to become horribly real.

"Ruby—" I started, but she tightened her grip around my arm.

"Don't," she whispered. "Not right now. Not here—okay?"

"Okay."

I understood that she didn't want to talk about it, but we needed to, whether she liked it or not. I would give her a reprieve for the moment—it wasn't like I wanted to have the conversation surrounded by nosy ministers, but I couldn't handle staying silent on this for long.

"We'll talk later?"

"Later," she replied.

I looked back over toward the dais. Jenney was standing by the steps, surrounded by young trainee ministers. She looked beautiful—out of her servant clothes and wearing something she'd most likely stolen from one of the guest rooms.

"She's going to have a different life from now on," Ruby mused as she followed my gaze.

"I hope so."

For all intents and purposes, Jenney was my younger sister. I hoped that while there would be countless negatives to being the king of Hellswan, one of the benefits would be the ability to spoil her rotten. I didn't want her going near a kitchen sink again, or working for so many hours that she ended up falling asleep on one of the kitchen chairs—something she did all too frequently. Maybe now she could actually start enjoying her life, making up for lost time...

"I hate to tell you this, but you'll be beating them off with a stick." Ruby tried to hide a smile, looking over at the fawning boys. "Sorry."

I grimaced as I assessed each of the hapless-looking ministers who surrounded her. I'd be keeping her away from *them* in the future—that was for sure.

"What's wrong with Julian?" I asked, noticing the boy watching the same tableaux we were, but scowling.

Ruby looked over at Julian standing in the corner of the room nearest the dais, skulking in the shadows. She sighed.

"When Benedict started to become influenced by the entity, I think he shut Julian out. Hazel and I were preoccupied all the time with the trials, and I think the only person who ever really paid Julian any attention was Jenney...I guess he thinks that's slipping away."

I understood how he felt. Would I be Julian soon, watching Ruby from afar because I couldn't have her, couldn't get close to her? Either way there would be distance between us—either we'd be like Hazel and Tejus, who had to physically distance themselves from one another to stop her draining him, or we'd be like Julian and Jenney, one of us standing on the sidelines while the other got on with their life.

"He still hasn't recovered, has he?" I replied, noticing his pallid features that were highlighted by the flickering candles of the room.

"No. He needs more rest, but I guess it's also psychological. He was down there for a long time, thinking that his friends had left him, not knowing if he would ever get out. That's got to leave a mark."

"We'll get revenge, Ruby," I reassured her. Queen Trina's time would come.

"I know," she replied, looking up at me with solemn

eyes. "I'm proud of you, by the way," she added. "King Ash of Hellswan."

I groaned.

"Don't—I'm Ash to you, Shortie, always."

She rose up on her tiptoes to kiss me lightly on the cheek. Unsatisfied, I drew her into a crushing bear hug, not wanting to let her go. I inhaled her familiar, warm Ruby smell that never ceased to drive me crazy.

"It's going to be okay, whatever happens," she whispered.

I nodded into her hair. Now I didn't want to talk about it—I just wanted to hold her, ignore the fact that I was a sentry and she was a human, that I was a king from a different dimension than hers, and that the castle I was supposed to protect with my life was already under threat from a powerful entity.

"Excuse me, your Highness."

Go away.

"Yes?" I replied, slowly lowering Ruby to the floor as I faced Lithan and Qentos.

"The trials are due to commence shortly." Lithan smiled, looking like a cobra about to strike. "New rule - no humans this time, and no Tejus. Just you."

Just me.

Great.

Let the games begin.

Ruby

After I'd said goodbye to Ash, we set off for the cove.

I was flying on the back of a vulture with Lieutenant Ragnhild. I had been initially surprised that he was joining us until he informed me that Ash had commanded that he go as my protector. I'd scoffed, telling the lieutenant that I really didn't need one, but secretly glad that Ash had thought to do something like that.

Tejus was flying with Julian, and Hazel was on her own bird, though it was being controlled by Tejus. It made the journey a bit slower, but it was the only way that we could be sure Hazel wouldn't start syphoning one of us mid-flight.

I knew it was for the good of us all, Hazel included, but it wasn't great seeing my friend being treated like she was a threat or a danger to us.

It will be you next.

The thought came unwelcome into my mind, and I shoved it away. I wasn't ready to contemplate that yet. I needed to talk it through with Ash...but I wasn't ready to do that either. I'd been teasing Hazel about her living in denial land, but clearly it was something that we were both experiencing in our own way.

I looked around at the aerial view of Nevertide as we began our descent. It was almost dusk now, and off in the horizon the sky burnt bright orange. I hoped Ash was okay. I didn't like not joining him for the trials. Even if I couldn't help, I wanted to be there. My imagination kept running away with me when I thought about the potential tasks the ancient ministers might put him through—the fact that Tejus had been so badly wounded he'd been unable to continue didn't fill me with confidence.

The vultures landed on a small cove covered in black rocks that jutted out from the sand. Lieutenant Ragnhild helped me off the bird, and I started to walk further up from the shore. I stared around in amazement at the bits and pieces of old Viking artifacts—half a rotted longboat, upturned chests and rusted weapons that had turned green with age.

"This is amazing," I murmured as Hazel came to walk beside me.

"I know. Tejus didn't know this was Viking stuff though—he said it was from the first sentries."

"Were the first sentries Vikings then?" I asked in amazement.

"Maybe." Hazel shrugged. "For all we know, Vikings could have been sentries. Might explain why they were so good at pillaging settlements…and why they were always described as so big."

"Huh, yeah—I guess so."

That would be an interesting development. It was possible, I supposed. They could have been the first to discover Nevertide. Maybe some of them settled here, though at least one account of them would mention syphoning abilities, surely?

My brain swirled with the possibilities. I hadn't really thought about the origin of the sentries before now. I just figured they had always existed only in this land, separate from the rest of both the supernatural and human dimensions.

"By the way," I interjected before I got completely sidetracked, "I spoke to Abelle at the coronation – she's a friend of Ash's, a bit like an apothecary I guess. Anyway, she said she might have some herbs that could help, stuff kids take when they're younger to stop syphoning."

Hazel look at me in surprise. "That sounds good…though a part of me thinks I should learn to control it by myself, not rely on medicines or whatever…"

I could see what she meant – it was better that Hazel had full control over her sentry abilities without relying on something to dull the effects.

"Think about it," I replied.

"I will… This is the way to the temple," Hazel announced as the earth started to dip down at the back of the cove as if there had been a landslide at some point, with tree roots left exposed along the walls of a small passageway. It led down to a solid stone door.

"He's in here?" I asked.

Hazel nodded.

Julian appeared at the top of the landslide, peering down at us. I beckoned to him—Benedict would want to hear his voice.

After Tejus used his True Sight to reassure Hazel that Benedict was in the temple, he and Lieutenant Ragnhild kept their distance, standing a few yards behind us.

"Benedict, it's Hazel—can you hear me?" Hazel placed her cheek against the stone, her palms flat on its surface. We waited for a few moments, and then I caught the sound of his voice.

"Hazel."

He sounded weak and frail, but it was definitely Benedict's voice. Hazel exhaled in relief.

"I'm here, I'm here. Are you okay?" she replied hastily.

"You shouldn't be here. It's late, isn't it?"

"That's okay—we'll leave before…well, you know."

"You should leave *now*." He sounded desperate.

"I'm not going to do that," Hazel replied firmly. "We're just going to stay and talk for a bit. It's okay. I've got Ruby here, and Julian."

"Julian?" Benedict asked.

"Yep, Queen Trina locked me up," Julian answered his friend. "But I'm out now…and soon, you'll be out, too."

"I'm glad you are," Benedict replied, sounding slightly more upbeat. "Hi, Ruby. Thanks for coming. How's Ash?"

"Well, Ash is king now, so that's cool," I replied with a smile.

"That's good. Ash will be a good king. Any other news I should know about?"

I looked at Hazel and she shook her head. I nodded in understanding. I was glad that we weren't going to have to tell Benedict that his sister was a sentry.

"That's it," Hazel replied with faux joviality.

"So you should go now, please—it would be better if you left. I don't know what will happen later…but I know it's coming."

I felt nauseated. Benedict was so frightened. I could hear it in his voice. I couldn't bear that he'd had to deal with this all by himself, being locked up in an underground temple for days, just waiting for some evil creature to start using him as its puppet whenever it felt like it.

"We'll go," Hazel agreed.

"Remember we all love you, Benedict."

I placed my hand on the stone in a goodbye gesture. A moment later, all three of us walked silently back to where Tejus and Ragnhild stood.

"Make yourselves comfortable," Tejus instructed. "We don't know how long we're going to have to wait."

I looked around for a comfortable spot, and settled against a grassy dune. There was very little light left in the day, and the moon's glow started to grow stronger above the ocean's horizon. Julian sat down on a rock, huddling against it and making his body as small as possible. I wondered if it had been a good idea to bring him—I partly felt like he should have remained at the castle, but he had been insistent. I also didn't know, in my heart of hearts, if Benedict was ever going to make it out of this. It was important for Julian to be able to speak to his friend, however briefly.

"I'm going to wait by the door," Hazel announced, standing up.

"No, you're not." Tejus corrected. "It's not safe."

"None of *you* are safe if I stay here. Benedict doesn't have much energy." Her voice wavered and she paused before continuing. "So it's nice to be near him—I don't get hungry."

Tejus was silent for a few moments.

"Fine," he snapped. "If I call you back, you come back, understood?"

"Understood."

Hazel strode back to the temple, her body tense with

misery and frustration. I hadn't realized how hard it had been for her being around us.

I shifted position in the dune, trying to get into a more comfortable spot. As I did so, I was reminded of the letter in my pocket as the paper crinkled against my robe. Pulling it out, I looked at the handwritten scrawl on the front. I wasn't sure if there was enough light to read it by, but it was worth giving it a try.

Varga.

I hated that he was gone.

Pulling open the envelope, I unfolded the letter. It was short, making up one side of the paper. Taking a deep breath, I began to read.

"Ruby,

Forgive me for this—I hope to deliver it myself, or tell you in person, but the chances are slim. I have halted my journey for a brief moment to write. Some may call that madness, but I know I am being followed and may not get out of this alive. As a dying man's last wish, please can you do me the great honor of passing on a message to Tejus that he won't want to hear? You are the only person left, with the exception of Tejus, whom I trust. Please make him listen to what you have to say. I am glad I will not have to take this to my death—it has weighed heavy on my heart for years.

As a young boy, I grew disillusioned with the way things were in Hellswan. Before my fifteenth year, Trina made me an attractive offer—the Acolytes. She promised power and riches beyond my imagining, and an understanding of my place in the world. We reformed the forgotten cult and kept ourselves secret, preparing for the day that the trials would commence. I will not divulge all the horrific things we did, just that I was responsible for Tejus and Trina Seraq starting a romantic relationship, pushing him in her direction as she asked. After a time, when he returned to his family and left her, I saw that he had done the honorable thing and I had not. Ashamed, disillusioned, I left the Acolytes.

They have wanted me dead for a long time. It seems it may finally come to pass.

I tell you this to warn you. All of you.

Their power and influence is far-reaching indeed. The members I know of include Lithan, who I believe to be still involved, and there will be other ministers too. Memenion's son I now believe is a member, and a number of villagers in Hellswan. I should have exposed them earlier, but I was threatened with my own exposure if I shared their secret. I was reassured that Tejus was so prone to hate and mistrust of those *within his castle, that he would be unlikely to overtly trust anyone who might pose a threat to him – I thought he would be safe. I was a coward, and I am profoundly sorry.*

There will be others. Trust no one.

Ruby, please don't hate me. I did what I did in my youth, and despise myself more than you ever could.

Tell Tejus that I never meant to betray him—he was my only friend, and I loved him as a brother.

Tell him to follow his heart.

Varga."

I re-read the letter several times.

I couldn't believe that Varga was one of the Acolyte members.

No!

I didn't *want* to believe it.

To me, Varga had been a knight in shining armor when I needed him most. I vowed that was the way I would remember him—courteous, honorable and a good man. He was not a coward—he had written this knowing full well that his friend might hate him for it, but also that it was necessary for our survival.

I looked over at Tejus.

I hated that I would need to pass on the message - that

I would be the one who would have to destroy the memories he had of his only friend. But I had no choice in the matter—the known members would have to be dealt with as swiftly as possible…and as for Queen Trina, well, her time was up as far as I was concerned.

Lithan.

He was no surprise…but he was also the minister at the trial right now, with Ash.

The thought made me queasy with fear and dread. What if Ash was walking into a trap? None of us even knew where he was…

"Tejus!" I called out. "I need to speak to you—*now!*"

ASH

Lithan and Qentos led the way to the pavilion. The remaining royals, Memenion, Hadalix and the abomination that was Queen Trina, were already gathered and waiting. I tried my hardest to avoid looking at the queen. Whenever I did, pictures of Julian's malnourished body would flicker through my mind, and I could recall Ruby's desperate cry for help when Queen Trina's barrier had come down around the cell. I didn't want to ever remember Ruby trapped and miserable like that, and I certainly would never let it happen again.

Each of the royals were permitted to bring a maximum

of two ministers from their kingdom with them. I had been one of Queen Trina's advisors, and I looked around to see who had been roped in as my replacement. As we got closer to the pavilion, I recognized a face—it was an older woman, one I'd never really spoken to much, who went by the name of Idiana. She was reputed to be tough, but also extremely intelligent…far more intelligent than the ministers of Hellswan, that was for sure.

Memenion greeted me with a nod as I stepped up to the pavilion, but Hadalix and the ministers ignored me completely. I could almost feel Queen Trina's gaze on me, no doubt mocking me, but I still refused to look in her direction.

"Kings and Queen of Nevertide." One of the Impartial Ministers stepped forward. "Today we fly to the Dauoa Forest to commence the trial."

What?

I heard the sharp inhale of our collective breaths. Had the ministers gone mad?

"What is the meaning of this?" Hadalix bellowed from beneath his arch.

The Impartial Minister didn't even bother looking in his direction—in fact, he wasn't looking at any of us, but straight ahead as if we weren't even there.

"You heard me. The Dauoa Forest. The integrity of the Imperial trials will not be questioned, King Hadalix. Not by any sentry here," he warned.

"The forest is forbidden!" Hadalix continued, ignoring the minister. "Not a soul has been in there in my lifetime. For good reason!"

"Rumors and myth, Hadalix. Have you let yourself be swayed by common talk?"

The king scoffed, but his face had drained of all its color. The rage was an act—it was mind-numbing fear that was making Hadalix speak as he did, and I didn't blame him.

I looked at Memenion questioningly. The king returned my gaze with a short shake of his head. Clearly this latest insanity of the ministers made no sense to him either.

"Did you learn nothing from the last time? More bloodshed on your hands—is that what you want?" Hadalix raged.

"We are not going to alter the traditions of centuries just because you are afraid," the minister replied. Queen Trina laughed cruelly. I hadn't seen her expression when the minister had announced our destination, but I wondered if she had already known. That, or she thought herself truly so powerful that the Dauoa could not harm her.

My father's old warning came back to haunt me.

The dead remain to whisper in the trees, boy—never venture into the Dauoa or you'll come back a half-creature, more demon than man.

The Dauoa had been forbidden to me and all the other children of Hellswan when I was younger. I had once, as a dare, approached its edges in broad daylight. Just standing there, staring into the gloom of the forest, I had felt as if I was being watched—as if the trees themselves were alive, their shadows and the thickets of their branches concealing whatever dark secrets the forest held inside.

It's just stories—fairytales and stories…

I wouldn't let fear get the better of me like Hadalix, and I wouldn't expose my weakness to the other champions or the ministers. I would find a way to survive this even if it felt like I was stepping into a death trap.

"If there are no further interruptions, we will fly to the Dauoa. Your ministers are welcome to join you, but you alone will be going into the forest."

With one last glare in Hadalix's direction, the minister turned on his heel and rejoined the rest of his ancient clan.

"An interesting location." Lithan sidled up to me. "They're certainly creative with their trials. I can't help but wonder if this is personally for your benefit, your highness."

"What do you mean?" I snapped.

He gave me a sickly smile.

"Just that. Perhaps they think you will back out—it looked like Hadalix was about to."

"Are you calling me a coward, Lithan?" I asked, more out of curiosity than actual anger. I knew I wasn't a coward, so if Lithan's comments were intended to strike a nerve, then they had failed.

"Not at all, your highness."

He'd managed to say 'your highness' like it was a slur. I turned away from him, ready to return to my vulture. Lithan's behavior was odd, even for him. If he wanted to continue working in the Hellswan ministry he had a funny way of showing it…which made me think that he had other plans.

Good.

I wanted to get rid of him as soon as possible. But I also

wanted to know where he'd be going. Lithan had been privy to a lot of Hellswan's secrets—both the emperor and Tejus had kept him close by at all times. If he was planning to become advisor at another kingdom—say, the Seraq kingdom—then something would need to be done.

Not caring whether Lithan and Qentos joined me or not, I jumped on my bird, ready to take flight.

We all flew up, hovering for a few moments around the pavilion, waiting for the Impartial Ministers to take the lead. The Dauoa forest was vast, entirely covering the northern lands of Nevertide. Not a single sentry lived there, nor was the forest ever used for timber supplies or hunting—as a result its geography remained a mystery to most of Nevertide's inhabitants.

The Impartial Ministers formed a 'v'-shaped flock and began to soar off. I followed with the rest, keeping my pace steady. I needed to have a moment alone—everything was happening so fast. It was only just starting to hit me that I'd been crowned this morning. Was I about to be the shortest-reigning monarch Hellswan ever had?

* * *

We touched down at the forest border, landing at the edge

of a vast, dried-out field of yellowing grass. Tall and imposing Okadale trees guarded the entrance. They looked ancient, and it occurred to me that whatever creatures were in that forest, they would be far older than any of us.

Even the vultures seemed jumpy. Many were squawking erratically, and shuffling back from where the trees' shadows cast the grass in gloom. The Impartial Ministers gathered together a few yards in front of the forest's edge, waiting impatiently for us to approach.

"Come, come!" one of them yelled, tapping on the ground with a gnarled wooden walking stick. I walked over. There wasn't any point in trying to delay the inevitable—we would be going into the forest whether I liked it or not.

"For centuries the emperors of Nevertide have descended to the Dauoa Forest to test their mettle against the most feared land in these kingdoms. Those who have returned usually find that there is little to truly fear other than fear itself—that beasts are beasts, wherever they may live. The courage and self-belief that you will find on completion of this task will carry you through your rule, should you succeed."

My eyebrows rose in surprise. For the Impartial Ministers, that speech was almost encouraging, and I wondered if their words belied the dangers that we would face.

"In the forest, there are four replicas of the emperor's scepter. The scepter signifies the emperor as a leader of his people, fashioned in the likeness of the shepherd's staff that the first emperor of Nevertide carried. You may use your powers freely once you enter, and there are no rules of engagement…but let me advise you this, those who turn on one another in the Dauoa never quite leave the spirit of the forest behind."

At the Impartial Minister's warning, I looked over at Queen Trina. She was staring into the dark depths of the trees beyond. At first I thought she was nervous, but then a gust of wind blew and she turned her face toward me. The look in her eyes was one of anticipation.

She's insane.

No one in their right mind would be looking forward to this.

Reluctantly, I headed toward the start of the forest.

"Ash, a moment, please."

I paused as King Memenion approached. He was

heavily armed, a mace hanging from his belt as well as the sword of his kingdom. On his back he wore a bow and arrow, and a small scythe had been buckled to his leg. My weaponry consisted of a dagger and the sword of Hellswan.

"Did you know we would be coming here today?" I asked, pointedly looking at his weaponry.

"No. But so far the trials have taught me nothing other than I should always come fully prepared."

I nodded. A heads up from Lithan or Qentos would have been nice, but really the shortcoming was mine—I should have known better.

"What would you say to traveling together, just for the first few miles?" Memenion asked. "It may increase our chances of survival. I don't know *what* is in there, but I do know we have less chance of defeating it alone."

I considered his proposal. There were four scepters in the forest, which meant that all those who returned with one would progress to the next trial. I didn't believe that Memenion would double-cross me—I didn't know the king well, but from what I had heard, he was a fair and just one. I also couldn't ignore the fact that he was much better prepared than I was. Only my pride held me back. Would I feel like I'd somehow cheated the task if I allowed

Memenion to accompany me? It wasn't like the trial at the lake…this was designed to be a solo venture.

Don't be a fool, Ash.

My pride would only leave me dead. Memenion's plan was a good one.

"I agree. We'll face whatever's in there together."

The king nodded, satisfied. He gazed at the forest in determination, his expression almost angry, like the place had personally offended him.

We carried on, walking side by side to our destination. As we reached the first tree, the temperature dropped significantly. I could have sworn I heard calls, soft, low whispers, coming from the darkness within, but I didn't know if it was just my imagination.

"Can you hear that?" I checked with Memenion.

He nodded. "Rumor has it that dead souls settle in the trees, waiting for the afterlife…but as I say, that's just rumor."

I nodded. "Just rumor. Right."

Memenion squared his shoulders, readying himself for whatever we were about to face.

"Let's go," I announced. We were wasting time. If night fell while we were in there we would risk getting completely lost. The forest was so large it could take days to find our way out.

We treaded as silently as we could through the undergrowth. I wrapped my traveling cloak around me more tightly as my breath came out in white vapors. I didn't understand the reason for such a temperature change. It was a warm day everywhere else across the kingdom.

We made good progress, walking briskly to keep warm, and heading in a northern direction. We had no clue as to where the scepters might be, but it would make sense that they'd be somewhere in the heart of the forest.

Memenion and I kept leaving markings on the trees with our daggers, hoping that they'd help us find the way back…that, or they'd lead something else right to us. But it was a risk we needed to take.

The whispers of the trees had continued as we walked. There was nothing discernible I could make out—it was more like a soft moan, sorrowful and unabating. I wished that it would stop. I felt like it would drive me mad before long, turning my own dagger on myself just to make the awful noise stop.

I should have been more careful what I wished for.

The whispering stopped suddenly, and Memenion turned to me in relief. We both grinned at each other. I took another few steps forward, and then froze. A resounding howl split the sudden silence.

"Fanged beasts?" Memenion whispered.

I don't think so.

It sounded a bit like them, the four-legged creatures that stalked most of the Hellswan forests and occasionally in winter dared to encroach on the cattle, but the cry was slightly different—lower, throatier, as if the creature was *larger.*

Another howl echoed, coming from a different part of the forest. We hadn't moved from where we stood, and soon the howls were coming with terrifying frequency— whatever these beasts were, there were lots of them.

"Do we run?" I suggested, my heart pounding in my chest as adrenaline kicked in.

"We'll make too much noise. They can probably smell us anyway. Perhaps it's better to stand our ground."

"Up ahead then," I agreed, pointing to a small clearing a few yards from where we stood. "At least we'll be able to see them coming."

Without hesitating, both of us rushed forward. As we

entered the clearing, we stood with our backs to one another, slowly circling as we faced the surrounding trees. It only took a moment before we heard the rustle of undergrowth—creatures moving steadily, stealthily toward us.

The thorn bush to my right shook, and I spun to face it head-on with my sword drawn and ready.

The blade tremored in my hand when I caught sight of the creature emerging from the undergrowth.

It was huge, the same size as a fully-grown fanged beast, but it was ghost white and severely malnourished—under a thin layer of short hair, I could see its bones sticking out at odd angles. Its jaws were large, the bottom half hanging down to show razor-sharp teeth as it drooled in my direction. Most horrifying of all were the eyes—they were completely white, as if the creature was constantly rolling them back in its head.

I stood still in terror, and felt Memenion do the same behind me. More of them appeared from the undergrowth, leering at us, panting and scratching at the floor as they waited to pounce.

Ash

Before I could take a moment to steady my shaking hand, they leapt at us.

Memenion roared as he lashed out with his blade, and I crouched low, ready to do the same. The creature landed in front of me, a forked tongue darting from its mouth, tasting the air. It reared up, the sharp blades of its teeth ready. I volleyed my sword upward, hitting the roof of its gaping mouth. The steel came into contact with brittle bone, and the tip of my blade came out the other side of its skull. It screeched, the rest of its body spasming in pain. With as much force as I could muster, I yanked the blade back out.

Before I could take a breath, another was upon me. While I fought it off, I could hear the neat splicing of arrows hitting their targets as Memenion fired one after the other into the undergrowth.

"There's too many!" he roared.

"I know!" I cried back. I had only injured the second creature. Another one was taking its place, with more snapping, waiting their turn behind. "We need a barrier— *now!*"

"We'll trap them in with us!" Memenion argued, flinging his bow to the floor and replacing it with his broadsword.

"We've got no choice," I panted as I released another volley of blows. "Do it—NOW!"

I flung the creature backward, and latched on to Memenion's mind as best I could. Our energy connected. Memenion's fear and rage met mine. The barrier emanated from us with a 'whoosh', knocking back most of the creatures as its clear blue light surrounded us. Two of the beasts remained.

Memenion and I made quick work of them— Memenion sending one of the creature's heads flying as he hacked at it with the scythe.

I slumped onto the ground, drained. I was covered with foul-smelling blood, a strange milky-red substance that turned my stomach.

"What the hell are they?" Memenion breathed as he collapsed on the ground beside me.

"The reason sane sentries avoid the Dauoa," I muttered.

The creatures were circling us, growling at the barrier and sniffing at its near-invisible wall, their forked tongues flickering in the air.

"You know, I think they're blind," I stated, remembering how the first creature had seemed to 'taste' the air before launching itself on me.

"You could be right," Memenion agreed, "though it doesn't make much difference. Their other senses are obviously heightened."

"I suppose we wait," I sighed, leaning back on my elbows.

Memenion nodded, about to lie down, but then he paused.

"Can you hear that?"

I listened, only hearing the sounds of the hungry growls.

"What?"

"Someone's coming this way," he replied. "I can hear footsteps."

I hoped it wasn't Hadalix. We couldn't shout out and warn him from the barrier, and unless he saw us first, he wouldn't know that he was about to stumble into a feeding frenzy.

Using True Sight, I followed Memenion's intent gaze. I didn't see anything for a few moments. I kept looking, and soon enough the distinct royal-blue robes of Queen Trina came into view.

"Queen Trina."

Memenion nodded, perceptibly relaxing.

"It will be an undeservedly swift end for her," he said with a grimace. I wasn't so sure. Queen Trina was deadly—and, though I hated to admit it, a far superior sword fighter than Memenion or me.

The creatures halted their sniffing of the barrier. One cocked their head inquisitively in the direction of Queen Trina.

Off you go then...for your next meal.

I willed the creatures to leave so that Memenion and I could continue our journey. They took off at a run, pounding the ground with their hooked claws. Turning back to Queen Trina, I watched her as she unwittingly continued forward.

I hoped the creatures *would* attack her. Whether they managed to defeat her or not, she deserved the unpleasant battle she had ahead of her.

A few moments later, the creatures were right on her tail, skulking through the undergrowth. As they drew closer, I started to look away—no matter how much I despised her, I wasn't macabre enough to want to witness her death. But before they could pounce, Queen Trina stopped. She waved a hand in the direction of the creatures, smiling beatifically.

What. The. Hell.

"Are you seeing this?" I hissed to Memenion.

The beasts started to emerge from the undergrowth, their heads down and their tails between their legs. They had instantly submitted to her.

"I don't understand…" Memenion spluttered.

We both watched in amazement as Queen Trina continued to walk on, the creatures following her like domesticated pets.

"What are they, her personal death hounds?" I snarled.

"I wouldn't put anything past her," Memenion

muttered. "And can you see how she's walking? She knows this forest, mark my words."

I watched. Queen Trina *did* have the air of someone who knew exactly where they were going. She sidestepped over a fallen log, raising her hand to catch a thorny branch and move it out of her way.

"You're right," I agreed. No doubt someone like Queen Trina felt perfectly at home in the Dauoa.

"I think we should follow her. It will get us to the scepters and out of here a lot faster," Memenion suggested.

I nodded. I didn't need to think twice. I wanted to know what other tricks Queen Trina had up her sleeve…and if she was a regular visitor to the Dauoa forest, I wanted to know why.

We broke through the protective barrier and hurried to catch up with her. We made too much noise, but it couldn't be helped—we'd lose her otherwise. I only hoped that the creatures were too entranced with their mistress to pay us any further attention.

As we got closer, we slowed down the pace, focusing on making as little sound as we could. The beasts following Trina eventually seemed to tire of their worship and started to trail off in the opposite direction. I heaved a sigh of relief when the last one disappeared into the thicket.

Trina started to hum softly to herself as she traveled through the forest. That, more than anything else, made my blood boil over. How *dare* she treat this task like it was nothing, like she knew she would emerge victorious? Memenion scowled—her jaunty little tune was obviously getting to him as well.

We followed her onward. Now the sun was starting to set, and what little light had been visible between the trees was fading to a red and orange glow.

Queen Trina stopped her humming, and I heard a giggle. At first I thought it was the queen, enjoying more of her leisure time in the forbidden forest, but it sounded too high-pitched to be coming from her.

Queen Trina stopped again.

"Out you come," she announced merrily.

I looked at Memenion in alarm.

Does she mean us?

Before I could move, or whisper to Memenion to run, little creatures started to emerge from the forest. They came from everywhere—scrambling down trees, appearing from burrows in the earth and out from under brambles.

They were *repulsive.*

Small, with little horns appearing out of their heads, the creatures were entirely green—and quite hairy. They crowded around Queen Trina while she cooed at them. One latched on to her leg, lovingly, looking in the direction of Memenion and me. We both ducked behind an old oak, my breath cut short as I prayed that it hadn't seen us. Peering around the trunk, I looked at the creature again. It was still staring in our direction, but perhaps it hadn't seen us – it didn't warn Queen Trina or the other creatures, so I continued to watch in silent horror as it danced around their mistress. Its eyes were black, beady little things and when it smiled, rows of sharp little pointed teeth appeared.

Goblins.

I remembered Ruby mentioning these creatures from the Hellswan brothers' trials. They were even more repulsive than I had imagined—Queen Trina's adoration of them didn't help. They squabbled with one another and played around her as she walked on, thankfully not noticing us following, but we now maintained more of a distance.

Finally, after a few more miles, we saw a golden glow in the distance. Looking more closely, I saw four scepters suspended in mid-air, hovering over stone plinths. No sooner had we seen them than we heard a loud crashing sound coming from behind us.

"It's Hadalix," Memenion breathed.

If that was the sound he'd been making throughout the forest all day, it was a miracle he was still alive. He stormed through the bushes and thorns that stood in his way, heaving a club left and right as he knocked down everything in his path.

The goblins fell silent. Then, as if there'd been some silent command that we couldn't hear, they scattered back into the undergrowth and disappeared from sight.

Queen Trina darted after them, changing direction.

What's she doing?

We were only a few yards away from the scepters...

I stayed with Memenion, both of us crouched down low, and watched as she walked silently back the way she'd just come, appearing right behind Hadalix a few moments later. They were only a few paces apart. Hadalix was making so much noise that he hadn't heard her approach.

She reached into the folds of her robe.

What in Nevertide is she doing...

"Look OUT!" I bellowed across the forest to Hadalix,

but I was too late.

Queen Trina had leapt up into the air, her dagger aimed for the king's back. He moved to turn just a split second too late. He screamed as the dagger plunged into his spine. Bright red blood splattered across Queen Trina's face as she smiled.

Hadalix's body crumpled pitifully to the ground.

Are we next?

Queen Trina looked up in my direction. I knew she could see me. Her smile became a laugh, and she waved.

"I think she knew we were following her the entire time," I breathed. Memenion didn't answer. His gaze was fixed on the body of Hadalix, blood slowly spreading across the back of his robe.

"She doesn't care that we know," I continued, outraged. "She thinks she's untouchable!"

She leapt over Hadalix's body, running ahead toward the golden glows of the scepters. When she was out of sight, we both rushed toward the body of the king.

"At least we have proof," I gasped. "The Impartial Ministers can't ignore this—her dagger's been left as well."

It had been plunged into his body to the hilt, the unmistakable crest of the Seraq kingdom carved into its ornate pommel.

"Let's carry him back. Forget the scepters," Memenion agreed. "Even if the ministers turn a blind eye, we have the evidence to bring her down. Not a soul in Nevertide will accept her rule as empress."

"You take the head," I replied, positioning myself at the other end.

As soon as Memenion bent down, I heard the menacing laughter of the goblins. They surrounded us, appearing as if they'd been lying in wait all along. I drew my blade as they approached.

They ignored us completely. Their little green bodies scurried forward, launching themselves on Hadalix till he was covered by a swarming green mass.

What are they doing?

"Get off!" I yelled, poking one of them with my sword.

"What are they…" Memenion trailed off as we heard the unmistakable sound of tearing flesh.

"Oh, no," I muttered.

They were eating him.

"ENOUGH!" bellowed Memenion, attacking them with his scythe. One of them grabbed the end of the blade as it came swooping toward them, and, yanking it out of

Memenion's grasp, threw it back onto the forest ground.

The sounds of their munching grew louder, accompanied by breaking bones and the slosh of Hadalix's organs being pulled out of place. *I'm going to be sick.*

I lifted my sword, ready to strike, but before I could bring it down on the fiendish monsters, they scattered.

"Oh, of all the things…" Memenion turned away from the body. It wasn't a pretty sight. There was certainly nothing left that resembled Hadalix—and the dagger had gone.

"Let's get the scepters."

Memenion nodded, picking up his discarded weapon, and walked on, not once looking back.

I didn't understand how Queen Trina had the audacity to be so brazen. Did she not care at all that we knew? Taking Ruby and Julian was one thing—if we'd exposed her for that, not many of the ministers would have batted an eyelid, and certainly not the Impartial Ministers. But killing a king was an entirely different matter. Queen Trina obviously thought she was above the law—above an attack from Memenion, me and Tejus, not to mention the entirety of Hadalix's kingdom. Did she think no one would believe us? Or, more worryingly, was Queen Trina accessing some kind of power that meant she no longer feared the blade of a sentry?

"Do we say anything to the Impartial Ministers?" I asked Memenion as we claimed our scepters.

"I no longer know." Memenion sighed. "It's what she expects us to do…"

"And she's no fool."

"Exactly."

If Queen Trina was happy for us to inform them of her deed, then there was really no point in doing it whatsoever.

We continued our journey back in silence. Soon we found the markings on the trees that we'd made on our way in and the whispering of the leaves returned. I couldn't *wait* to leave this forest.

I had one more question for Memenion before we exited the forest. I just didn't know how much I trusted him. It wasn't his actions that made me question him, more that this was Nevertide, and if I'd learnt anything over the last few days it was not to trust a single soul in this land till they'd proven themselves worthy of it. But perhaps Memenion had. Tejus trusted him, at least, and despite my personal opinion of Tejus, he now counted as one of the few I *did* trust—besides Ruby.

'The Impartial Ministers," I blurted out before I could change my mind. "Do you think they're involved in this? Do you think they're assisting Trina's rise to empress?"

"Be careful who you share that opinion with," Memenion snapped at me. "But yes, I do. I can't really make sense of her flaunting her treachery otherwise. Even without proof, the word of a king would ordinarily prompt an investigation at the very least. But in this case I doubt that's going to happen."

"Maybe we *should* tell them, then," I replied. "If they knew her plan, and she tells them that we saw her kill Hadalix, then it will look suspicious if we don't say anything – like we suspect them of being in league with her."

"Good point," Memenion grunted. "Let me do it— they'll pay no attention to you."

I nodded, knowing that he didn't mean the words unkindly. It was perfectly true—the Impartial Ministers didn't see me as a valid champion—but that didn't matter to me. Once it would have—it would have mattered a *lot*—but now I only cared about ensuring Queen Trina never got anywhere near that crown.

"I'll let Tejus know. I think it's time Queen Trina got a

taste of her own medicine," I replied.

"I don't know if I'd trust Tejus to be the one to do it," Memenion replied. "He may deny it now, but he loved her once. He'll find revenge harder than he thinks."

I turned to the king in surprise, and he gave me a level look.

"Just heed what I say," he replied simply. "Matters of the heart are never as straightforward as we think."

We took our last steps out of the forest, holding our scepters aloft. The Impartial Ministers stood off in the distance. Queen Trina was not among them – she'd either left already or continued petting her creatures in the forest. They politely clapped our success as we drew closer, but all I could see on their faces was the smug satisfaction of treachery and betrayal.

You'll pay for this too, I thought to myself. *All of you will pay, eventually.*

I turned away from the ministers in disgust, letting Memenion explain what we'd seen in the forest. I heard the skepticism in their voices, but eventually a few of them returned to the Dauoa to investigate. I waited with Memenion – knowing that it was pointless. Undoubtedly, they would return to say it was a goblin attack, without any evidence of Queen Trina being involved. But if we were to keep up the charade, then we should play our part – if we could convince the Queen that we were dumb enough to believe the Impartial Ministers were keeping these trials fair and unbiased, then hopefully we'd stay a step ahead of her…

A few hours later, the Impartial Ministers returned from the shadows of the forest. They approached us slowly – their heads downcast and grim.

Is that an act?

I couldn't tell. We waited for them to speak, to give their verdict of Hadalix's death. The fact that they hadn't returned with his body suggested to me that there probably wasn't much left of it to return *with*.

"Goblins," said one. "That was Hadalix's fate. You accuse the Queen unjustly, Memenion and Ashbik. We shall hear no more of your folly – let the dead rest in peace."

I met the eyes of the minister. He gazed back at me, unfazed. Perhaps he *did* believe what he was saying.

"Let us leave, Ashbik," Memenion muttered so only I could hear. "These ministers are either lying or stupid, or both."

"Queen Trina?" I questioned before we left. "Has she emerged yet?"

"Before either of you, yes," another minister replied. He glared at me reproachfully, as if I shouldn't be questioning them – or her.

"Fine," I spat, before joining Memenion. As we strode away from the forest, I now had serious concerns about the outcome of the trials – the ministers were clearly against me winning. If they wanted me out of the running it would be all too easy for them to achieve that – and make it look like an accident. It seemed that Memenion would be Nevertide's only hope in keeping Imperial power away from the clutches of Queen Trina.

Tejus

The wait was intolerable.

All I could do was stare silently at Hazel as she curled up in a ball by the entrance to the temple. I wanted to comfort her, to hold her, but I couldn't risk being syphoned before Benedict emerged. I would leave her exposed to danger that way. As it was, I was having a hard time forgiving myself for what I'd caused her to become. Seeing her around her friends was difficult – I knew that in time it would change, but I would do anything to spare her the agony of the growing period she was about to experience as she came into her powers and gradually learned to harness them.

"Tejus!"

I turned to see Ruby hurrying toward me.

"I need to speak to you—*now!*"

Glancing back at Hazel, I waited for her to react to the shouts of her friend, but when she made no movement, I realized she was asleep. It was probably for the best. I just had to keep in mind that she would probably wake up hungry.

"What is it?" I snapped. Julian and Ragnhild were looking over in our direction, waiting curiously for Ruby to divulge whatever was bothering her. Instead of speaking, she shoved a letter into my hand.

I was about to ask her what it was when I noticed the familiar handwriting. It belonged to Varga—what was Ruby doing with a letter from him? Without saying another word, I began to read what he had written.

When I finished, I crumpled the paper into my fist. It needed to be burnt before anyone else saw it.

"I thought he was a good man—at the end of it all," Ruby whispered.

I didn't trust myself to speak.

"He was just misguided," she continued, "but he loved

you like a brother."

"You don't know what you're talking about," I spat out. I didn't want to hear Ruby's opinion on the betrayal of my only friend. How insidious and sickening Queen Trina's grip had been on him—on both of us.

"Forgive him, Tejus," she urged. "I don't believe he ever meant you harm."

"You don't?" I asked her.

"No!" she stated. "I just think he lost his way. And I don't think he's the only one guilty of *that*."

At the damning insult, she flounced back to where she'd been sitting, avoiding the wide-eyed stare of Julian, who had witnessed the exchange.

Ignoring them all, I strode purposefully toward the water's edge. The tide was out, leaving the damp sand littered with the debris of the sea—the bleached skeletons of its long-dead inhabitants, the soft sludge of underwater weeds and the stench of rot.

I cursed my friend. The initial betrayal I could forgive—Queen Trina was a snake, capable of worming her way into the lives of anyone she wished, polluting their minds till they turned on friend and family alike. It was the years of silence that wounded me the most. He *had* been a coward—why had he never told me?

Would you have ever spoken to him again if he had?

Would you have banished him?

Exposed him?

Perhaps. It was too late to know for certain. I wanted to think that I wouldn't have, that I would have forgiven him…but I could not say for sure. I had never managed to forgive my brother anything, so why would Varga have been any different?

Frustrated, I unfurled the letter again.

I should have known that Lithan was up to no good. I had suspected him of disloyalty, but the harmless, gossiping kind. I had been very careful to keep him close, but not to divulge anything that could damage my family or me. I hadn't realized the true nature of his treachery…I had been too conceited, too arrogant to believe that he could do me any real harm.

Fool, I cursed myself.

My eyes were drawn back to the letter, Varga admitting that he had brought Queen Trina and me together at her insistence. How shameful that I had been so easily manipulated. I recalled how Varga had always encouraged it in the beginning, urging me to visit her, accompanying me to the palace time and time again…how I had supposed that we were all friends, not for a moment thinking I was the fly in some kind of intricately woven web.

There had been one night that I now remembered with clarity. Trina often left our bed in the middle of the night—she claimed that she had trouble sleeping, and I never questioned it, as I was always happy to sleep alone. She would return at dawn, sleepy and doe-eyed, curling up to me. Once I had heard her and Varga talking outside the bedroom door before she returned, but I had thought nothing of it—it had been near the end of our relationship, and I had started to care less about what Trina said or did. I wondered now if they had been returning from an Acolyte meeting…if that was where she had been going every night—where they had *both* been going.

The thought made me feel sick.

My mind was brought back to the present as a faint green glow had started to emanate from behind me.

"Ruby!" I called out, already running toward the temple. "Get Hazel away from there!"

I saw the blonde girl scurrying across the sand. As I reached the entrance, Hazel and Ruby were already slowly backing away from the stone door.

"Get behind me," I growled at Hazel, resisting the urge to yank her back. Both of them moved swiftly, joining Julian and Ragnhild in the cover of the trees. The door had started to tremor in its setting, causing the ground to rumble with a low, intense shudder. Slowly the door started to grind sideways, and more green light spilled from the entrance, lighting up the path.

The silhouette of Benedict was slowly revealed. He stood, patiently waiting, statue still, as the door opened fully. He moved forward, his steps slow and unhurried as he ascended the slope of the path.

"B-Benedict?" Hazel whispered. I held up my hand in warning—I wanted her to be silent. Whatever Benedict was about to do, I wanted him to do it without being interrupted...I *needed* to know more, and this was our only chance.

I hastily backed away, avoiding the glare of the green light. I didn't know if he knew we were there or not—sometimes when we'd encountered him under possession he appeared to be completely oblivious to our presence, and then sometimes not.

Silently, I watched as he turned in the direction of the

water. He moved steadily over the rocks and dunes, avoiding the remains of the ships. As he moved out of the intensity of the light, I realized that he was clutching one of the stones in his hand. It glowed softly. It meant that Benedict would be strong right now. We had to be careful.

I edged forward, wondering what he was doing. He looked as if he was heading straight for the sea…

He was. He walked swiftly over the sand where the tide had gone out, but didn't stop when he got to the water, wading straight in, his splashes echoing through the absolute silence of the cove.

Is the entity trying to drown him?

Hazel had obviously reached the same conclusion I had.

"Benedict, no!" she cried out, running out from the trees to follow him. I grabbed her as she tried to run past me.

"Hazel, stop!"

The searing pain of her syphon flooded my body, disorientating me with pulsing shocks like someone was digging pins into my brain matter, but I held on, not willing to let her anywhere near her brother. Knowing she would hate me for it later.

My grip tightened.

"Come back!" she screamed, and I held my hand over her mouth, willing her to be quiet.

While she struggled in my arms Benedict waded into the water up to his waist. He paused, waiting for something, and then raised his arm in the air, holding the stone aloft. Hazel stopped struggling.

With an almost careless flick of his arm, the stone went flying into the water. I heard the heavy 'plop' as it hit the surface, sinking to the bottom of the ocean. I waited, looking out to the sea…*what's supposed to happen?*

Benedict lowered his arm and started to walk back toward the shore.

"Don't move," I commanded in Hazel's ear, gritting my teeth against the pain. I released her, praying she would do as I asked. This was our chance to restrain him—if the stone had left his possession he should be in a weakened state…

"Ragnhild! A barrier!" I cried, needing the extra mental strength the guard would provide after holding onto Hazel. He ran toward me, throwing out his energy. It wasn't very strong, not what I would expect from a lieutenant, but our energy linked nonetheless.

I was about to throw the barrier outward, but before I

could focus, Benedict stumbled on a rock. Rather than righting himself, his body fell forward, collapsing onto the sand.

"BENEDICT!"

Hazel started to run, and I didn't have the energy to stop her.

ROSE

We stood around the portal, suspended inches from the surface of the water. The black tar-like substance hadn't moved, despite the witches and the jinn working their magic on it for hours.

"This is impossible!" declared Aisha. "I've never even seen this black stuff before. It's gross."

I rolled my eyes. This wasn't the first tirade of complaint that Aisha had exploded with, and if this continued much longer, it wouldn't be the last.

"Patience, girl," Nuriya scolded. "Go back to the moldy drinking hole if you want."

"No, thanks," Aisha retorted. "It stinks like wet dog."

Corrine sighed irritably—Aisha had broken her concentration. The witch looked downhearted, and I started to worry. *Really* worry. What if we could never get it open? Given all that I'd survived in my life, I'd kind of always believed that where there was a will, there was a way…but it didn't look like all the will in the world was having much luck here.

"Maybe we need to head back." Corrine exhaled. "I don't know how much difference we're making. If we could find out more about it, where it might lead, we might have more luck."

Mona opened her eyes—she'd been in a trance-like state, not remotely bothered by the constant whining of Aisha.

"Corrine is right. We've tried everything—"

Mona went silent as the tar of the portal shifted. We all looked down at its black, shiny surface. It was still. Had we imagined it? No…it shifted again, the surface jolting, like something behind it was trying to get out.

With a sludgy groan, the tar moved again. This time something burst from its center, shooting up into the air and then abruptly falling back down again, missing the portal, instantly being swallowed by the sea.

"What the hell was that?" I asked.

"No idea…I'm about to find out," Corrine whispered.

She placed her hands over the surface of the water, closing her eyes for a few moments. There was a fizzing on the sea's surface, white foam quickly swirling in a mini-tornado. The water rose up, reaching the tips of Corrine's fingers. Balanced on its surface was a small, dark stone.

Corrine picked it up, and the water collapsed back down.

We all stared at it in silence.

It had a kind of reddish tint, and was almost perfectly round. Maybe it was a jewel of some kind? But it looked a little too dull for that. Before I could ask any questions, Nuriya tentatively took it out of Corrine's hands and held it up to the light.

"Do you know what it is?" I asked.

The jinni's face looked quizzical, but it was a few moments before she answered me.

"I think I do…" she murmured, then broke off into silence once again.

"Well?" demanded Aisha, echoing all of our thoughts.

"Long ago," Nuriya began, wetting her lips, "and we are

talking thousands of years, the jinn had an ancient practice of binding the souls of malevolent supernatural creatures into stones… stones just like this one."

"Any creatures?" I probed.

"Yes…but there was one in particular. I can't recall what it was, but the stone would bind them from doing harm. The stones were placed in the In-Between—there's a star full of them, every single part of it covered with these stones, each holding a soul that's been locked away for eternity." She lowered the stone, handing it back to Corrine. "We need to put this in a bag. The stones are powerful things—they can send even supernaturals mad if exposed to them for too long."

Corrine tightened her fingers around it, staring at Nuriya.

"Corrine?" I prompted, waiting for the witch to procure a bag.

"It's powerful," she whispered, moving the stone around in her palm.

Nuriya and I looked at one another.

Aisha leaned forward, knocking the stone out of Corrine's hand and catching it before it fell back into the water.

"Well, that proves *that* theory." She rolled her eyes and placed the stone in one of the pockets of my backpack.

Corrine seemed to shake herself awake. "That was scary," she said, looking stunned—something I wasn't used to from Corrine. "The stone…it felt like it was *calling* to me."

"Don't touch it again," Mona replied quickly. "None of us touch it if we can help it."

We all nodded, some of the less powerful witches still staring at Corrine in bewilderment. If Corrine could be swayed by its call, and Mona was warning us against it, then I didn't have much hope of any of us being able to handle its power.

"Can we use the stones to unlock the portal?" Corrine asked. "They're obviously powerful. If we can get enough, perhaps it will be enough power to dislodge the block?"

"It's worth a try." Nuriya nodded. "As I said, the stones are powerful. The energy contained within them might provide us with enough force to amplify our magic on the portal."

"Won't we be in danger of opening the stones?" Mona asked. "Releasing whatever's inside them?"

Nuriya shook her head. "It's doubtful that we will be

able to open them, even if we wanted to – the stones are sealed with a much more powerful magic than ours…the stones are ancient, and whatever locked them is long lost to us now."

The jinni looked thoughtful, and we waited in silence for her to continue.

"It would mean that we would have to travel to the In-Between. I haven't been there in a while…" she resumed softly.

"Can we not try with just the one stone?" I asked, not wanting to leave the portal for a second when I felt that we were so close to making a breakthrough.

"One is not enough," Nuriya replied. "The magic of the portal lock exceeds the magic of a single stone—it must be equally weighted if this is to work."

"So we go to the In-Between," Mona announced.

"And face an entire planet of stones like the one that just sent Corrine into total crazy-space?" Aisha retorted. "That doesn't seem very smart."

"We don't really have a choice," I reminded her.

Aisha exchanged a glance with her husband Horatio, then frowned, staring wearily at my backpack. I understood the woman's misgivings—I shared them, but for the first time since we'd found the portal I also felt hopeful. If a bunch of stones were the key to unlocking the portal, then I would stop at nothing to get my hands on them. I also desperately wanted to know what kind of creature was so dangerous to the jinn that rather than killing them, they locked them in eternal stone prisons. Could they even *be* killed? If those were the creatures waiting on the other side of the portal, then my kids were in more danger than I could even contemplate.

"Caleb," I breathed. My chest had suddenly tightened, and I felt the back of my neck breaking out in perspiration. This was not good.

"Don't jump to conclusions," he replied firmly.

"Caleb's right," Corrine replied. "We don't know anything yet—just that there's a distinct possibility that someone on the other side of the portal wants us to get in."

I nodded.

Please be one of the kids.

Maybe it was a message? Both Hazel and Benedict knew about the story of Mona, Kiev and the rest of Matteo's crew being released from a stiff portal by Benjamin and Abby. If they realized that the portal out of their dimension was blocked, then they would know what to do.

I tried to force myself to calm down and then addressed the group.

"Let's head back to the port and call the others. Then we're taking a trip to the In-Between."

HAZEL

His body lay in the sand, his face ghostly pale and everything about him looking crumpled and broken.

How did this happen?

How did I let *this happen?*

I couldn't even touch him without causing him more pain. Ruby turned him over gently till he lay on his back. She leaned forward, pressing the side of her face to his chest. Julian sat on the sand, clutching at the hand of his friend.

"I can feel a heartbeat," she whispered. "It's faint, but it's there."

I nodded, feeling dizzy with relief. I was grateful that Ruby was here, being the responsible sister when I was incapable of anything other than overwhelming hunger. I focused on doing what I could - hastily removing my robe and placing it around Benedict.

"We need to move him," I muttered. "He needs to get away from this place."

"I'll take him back with Ragnhild."

"Let me get Tejus—we should all go back together," I replied, looking around for both him and the lieutenant. I couldn't see them anywhere. "Where's—"

As soon the words were out of my mouth, Tejus barked my name. "Hazel, the temple," he called out, his voice echoing from the hollows of the earth.

I hesitated, looking down at Benedict.

"Go. I'll look after him," Ruby replied. "If we don't discover more about the entity, soon, we're all in trouble."

I nodded, staggered to my feet and ran down to the temple. The door had remained open after Benedict emerged, and the eerie green light still spewed from its depths.

Ragnhild and Tejus were both peering over the stone table block in the center, where the light was strongest.

Flickering within the green light, the brightly multi-colored stones from the Hellswan locks danced erratically in their settings.

"All the grooves are filled," Tejus muttered as I walked over to stand at the opposite side of the table. As soon as I'd entered the temple, hunger had kicked in—I could feel my throat constricting, and a dull hollowness in my stomach. I still didn't truly understand why the effects of mind hunger felt so *physical*, like my body was in the throes of starvation.

Doing my best to ignore it, and mentally block Tejus, I looked down at the surface of the table. All the grooves were filled but one.

"Do you think that's the stone that Benedict just threw in the water?" I asked, placing my finger over the empty groove. It felt warm.

Tejus nodded. I looked up at him—waiting for answers. *What does this mean? How much danger are we in?*

His mouth was set in a line, his dark brows furrowed. The light that emanated from the runes in the table and the stones cast part of his face in a green glow, while the rest remained shadowed. The effect made the stark planes of his face sharper and more prominent. I'd been about as intimate as anyone could get with this man, but as I stared at him, hoping for words of reassurance or hope, I felt like I was looking at a stranger.

"Is the entity free now?" I whispered.

"I don't know."

None of us knew enough. I felt like we were completely unprepared despite the fact that we'd been hurtling toward this inevitability ever since the emperor had taken the stone and placed it in the Hellswan sword. One action—one seemingly insignificant action—taken by a foolish, arrogant old man, and now we were facing a terrifying and uncertain future.

I looked around the temple. Nothing *felt* that different. If anything, since Benedict had collected the last stone, Hellswan had felt almost peaceful…if you didn't count me trying to syphon off my friends.

"We should return to the castle," Lieutenant Ragnhild announced, his fingers tracing the glowing runes that surrounded the table. "If the entity is coming, then we should all be somewhere safe."

I didn't know how *safe* I considered Hellswan castle, but I was eager to get Benedict away from here.

"Tejus, will you take Benedict?"

I had agreed with Ruby when she'd suggested that Ragnhild take Benedict, but I realized that there was no one else I trusted with my brother's safety. Tejus would protect him with his life—and anything less than that was unacceptable to me right now.

"Of course," he replied.

We walked out of the temple, and made our way over to Ruby and Julian, who were still hovering over my brother. Ruby was stroking his forehead and muttering to him.

"How is he?" I asked.

"I think better—his heartbeat's getting stronger," Ruby replied, smiling up at me. "I think he's going to be all right."

Suddenly I felt lighter, and along with an overwhelming surge of love for my friend, my perspective shifted. The uncertainty and fear around the rising of the entity suddenly felt manageable. Maybe it was the peaceful night and the stars shining down on us that encouraged my optimism, but I felt like the danger had abated—and as long as my friends were alive and well, and we were together, then we could overcome the obstacles Nevertide threw our way.

"Tejus is going to take him back," I replied, smiling back at Ruby.

"Okay," she replied, and both she and Julian backed away from Benedict so that Tejus could pick him up. He bent down, cradling Benedict's head in the crook of one arm while the other went under his knees. Rising, he held my brother against his chest as if he weighed about as much as a bag of feathers.

"Thank you," I sighed, my insides turning to goo.

He nodded, and turned toward the water. The vultures had reappeared on the shore, and Lieutenant Ragnhild stood waiting with them. He was shifting from foot to foot with impatience. I assumed that he was eager to get the castle on security lockdown, as I belatedly realized that the guards and ministers would have no idea that the entity had seemingly completed the unlocking of his own prison.

We all climbed onto the birds, and soon the cove and its unnatural green glow was out of sight. I hoped I would never have to return to that place; I never wanted to see that temple again—I never wanted to be in the presence of something built for the sole purpose of worshiping something so dark and evil.

I couldn't see much of Nevertide as we soared back

toward the castle; most of the land was in complete darkness, other than the small clusters of light still burning in the villages and the almost welcoming glow coming from the windows of Hellswan castle.

We landed in the courtyard of the castle. Two of the guards waiting at the door strode forward to greet us. I thought they were coming to receive their orders from Tejus, and I was momentarily surprised when he didn't start barking out commands…

Right. No longer king.

That would take some getting used to.

Lieutenant Ragnhild took over, instructing the men to step up their security detail, but without divulging what we'd discovered in the temple. The guards didn't ask any questions, and hurried off to do his bidding.

"I'll take him to the human quarters," Tejus said to Ruby and me. "You'll need ministers to aid him though. Tell Ash when he returns from the trials, if he's not back already."

"I don't want ministers near him," Ruby interjected, and I looked at her in surprise—I completely agreed, but it was usually *me* being stubborn about the ministers.

"I'll let Ash know who's safe," Tejus replied. "You

might need one, trust me on this."

"What do you mean?" I asked. There was something going on here that I didn't quite understand.

"Do you have the letter?" Ruby asked Tejus as we hurried along the main hallway.

What letter?

"No." His reply was abrupt, and he avoided making eye contact, picking up the pace as if he wanted to outrun both of us.

I looked over at Ruby; she grimaced and shook her head. I sighed. This was clearly a conversation to have at another time.

Whatever it was, it could wait. I wanted Benedict somewhere warm first. Two guards were stationed outside the human quarters. They stood aside hurriedly as we approached, staring disbelievingly at Benedict cradled in Tejus's arms.

He probably syphoned off them at some point.

I realized that there would be few sentries in Hellswan who hadn't been syphoned by the entity-possessed Benedict. I hoped that they all understood he hadn't been in control, hadn't known what he was doing at the time. I dreaded one of the guards or ministers confronting him. It was probably a good idea that I had a word with Ash when I next saw him about keeping Benedict shielded from the worst of his night-time activities in Hellswan.

"Oh, my God!" Yelena rose from where she'd been seated in the living room, her eyes widening as Benedict was carried toward her.

Tejus placed him gently down on the sofa, and Yelena crouched down low next to him.

"What happened? Is he sleeping—can I do anything?" She rattled off questions, and I recognized the same mixture of relief and anxiety that I was experiencing at seeing my brother finally free from the entity.

"We're going to get one of the ministers to see what they can do. I think he's just a bit weak," Ruby replied. "The entity took a lot out of him."

Yelena's face fell.

"But right now he probably just wants to be kept warm—and maybe you could keep him company?" I asked, suddenly *needing* Yelena to remain optimistic. I wanted Benedict to feel safe and secure when he woke, and that wasn't going to happen if we were all staring worriedly and tiptoeing around him.

It worked. Yelena brightened again, and went about

fetching more blankets for the sofa.

"I need to leave," I whispered to Tejus.

The hunger was starting to get to me. I could practically feel the energy of the kids emanating from the bedrooms—they felt like they were getting stronger every passing second, and the ache in my stomach was starting to become unbearable. Spending time with Tejus wasn't much better, but at least I knew he could handle whatever I threw his way.

Tejus's expression was instantly concerned, and he turned to Ruby. "Tell Ash that Lemidea is probably the best minister for this." He gestured toward Benedict. "We need to know if he's truly free of the entity. She's a good healer, and we can trust her."

"As far as you know," Ruby shot back.

"As far as any of us can know," he replied firmly. "Just pass on the message."

Ruby nodded.

"Fine."

Tejus and I left after saying a brief goodbye—I figured everyone could sense my increasing discomfort. I left feeling ashamed. Like I was separate from them all now, my newfound abilities creating a divide that I wasn't sure

I was ever going to be able to overcome, whether or not my syphoning urges got under control.

I'm a sentry.

I'm a SENTRY.

Reality hit me hard. Bulldozer hard. I kept walking, dully following Tejus back along the corridor and up the staircase to his room. My mind became a total whirl of questions and worries.

What if I never get it under control?

Will I have to stay in Nevertide forever?

What are Mom and Dad going to say?

What is Benedict going to say when he wakes?

Will I ever have a normal life again…or 'normal' for me, anyway?

My brief interlude of optimism came crashing to the floor, and as we came closer to the living room door, I started to have trouble putting one foot in front of the other. I felt trapped, claustrophobic, like the walls were closing in on me, and I was stuck dealing with the consequences of choices I hadn't really made.

"You need to take a breath, Hazel."

I looked up at Tejus. His tone had been firm, but his eyes betrayed uncertainty…about me, about us, about what was coming—I couldn't tell.

"I'm sorry," I breathed, "I think reality just hit…"

"I understand, but try and keep some perspective…One day perhaps you'll be glad of your abilities – it's not a death sentence, Hazel. It's not even a Nevertide life sentence – just because you're a sentry, it doesn't mean you'll have to stay here forever if you don't want to."

"I know," I whispered, suddenly saddened by his words…did he mean that he would be letting me go? Leave Nevertide without him? I wasn't sure.

I looked away, and we continued walking to the door. Tejus paused before opening it, and turned back around to face me. His expression had changed, his eyes hooded and dark.

"I can handle it. It's worth it," he whispered.

His arms abruptly circled me, fiercely pulling us closer together. I felt the hunger consume me, but it was different this time—flickers of something more human and needy erupted from the pit of my stomach. When Tejus lowered his lips down to meet mine, I responded greedily, the kiss deepening and dragging every last breath out of me. I reached up, winding my fingers into his dark hair, not allowing an inch of space between us.

I felt the syphon start, Tejus's energy becoming mine as not just my mind, but every single cell in my body took what was his. It must have hurt, but he didn't release me.

"I'm sorry," I whispered raggedly, tearing our lips apart. "The fault is mine, and mine only."

Tejus held me tighter, kissing me again.

Ruby

Jenney and I sat in the kitchen, waiting for a broth to boil that she was making for when Benedict awoke. We sat in the easy chair by the fire, both cradling cups of a Nevertide version of herbal tea—it tasted pretty revolting to me, but I didn't have the heart to tell Jenney that, and at least it was warm.

"How's Hazel holding up?" she asked, breaking the sleepy silence that had settled over us both.

"She's kind of pretending everything's okay, but I'm not entirely convinced. She's not able to be near any of us comfortably—not even Tejus. I don't see how she *could* be fine."

Jenney nodded, her forehead creasing in concern. Our silence resumed, both locked in our own thoughts and concerns. I guessed that Jenney was equally anxious for Ash to return from the trials. He should have been back by now, surely?

I looked around the kitchen, thinking about the time when Ash and I had first tried to practice our mind melds. It felt like a lifetime ago. So much had changed since then, so much had happened.

"Jenney," I asked suddenly, "why are you still in here?"

"What do you mean?" she replied.

"The kitchen...aren't you kind of free from this now? Able to be a lady of leisure now that your theoretical brother is king?"

Jenney smiled shyly, shaking her head.

"I wouldn't know what else to do. And do you see any other kitchen staff around here?" she asked. "Most of them have gone back to the village or sought refuge in Memenion's kingdom—no one thinks Hellswan is safe anymore. If I wasn't in here, we'd all starve."

"Why didn't you say anything?" I exclaimed. "How have you been doing this all on your own?"

"Yelena helps," she replied. "So do the other kids—don't worry about it, Ruby, honestly."

I was about to protest, tell her that she needed to tell Ash. I knew for sure that he didn't know what was going on, and I didn't think he'd be pleased when he found out. Before I could open my mouth, Ash walked into the kitchen.

"Ash!" I jumped up from the chair, so happy to see that he was all in one piece.

"Hey," he answered wearily, discarding an impressive-looking golden scepter on the kitchen table with a bang.

"So the trial went well?" I asked, eyeing the scepter. It didn't look like a booby prize...but Ash was clearly in a bad mood.

"I'm not knocked out of the running"—he sighed wearily—"but it was *not* good."

Jenney and I listened open-mouthed as he told us what had happened in the Dauoa Forest. I wasn't remotely surprised at the actions of Queen Trina, but when Ash told me that the ministers hadn't seemed to care remotely about what happened to Hadalix, I felt a cold chill run down my spine. If they were taking such a cavalier attitude toward deaths during the trial, then there would be no reason why Ash couldn't be targeted next.

"She's got to be stopped," I replied. "This has gone on long enough. We keep saying that we're going to get even, me included, but Queen Trina just seems to get away with *everything*. I thought Tejus would have done something by now—I mean, surely she's done enough to warrant getting locked up in a dungeon of her own?"

Ash pulled a face. "Yeah…Memenion mentioned something about that…that Tejus might not be so willing to get revenge on account of their past. This is something that might be left up to us, which is not such a bad thing."

"Do you think that's true about Tejus?" I asked worriedly. He couldn't possibly still have feelings for her, could he? He is in love with Hazel…

"I don't know." Ash shrugged. "But it hardly matters now anyway. That woman's reign is going to come to an end, and very soon. At least Memenion's on our side."

I nodded, not entirely focused on what he was saying - still distracted by Memenion's comments.

"Did you see Benedict?" Ash asked, changing the subject.

"Better than that." I managed a lopsided grin. "He's in the castle—and, as far as we can make out, free from the entity too."

Now it was my turn to share news. I told him about the trip to the Viking graveyard, and what had happened with Benedict. I also told him about the contents of Varga's letter—and at that, Ash's face became drawn and tight.

"I knew Lithan was up to no good!" he exploded. "I want him out of this kingdom *tonight*. Tejus chose to keep his enemies close, but I won't make the same mistake."

"I understand," I replied calmly, "but I've been giving it some thought. We know next to nothing about the Acolytes—who they are, what their part has been in the rise of the entity, if any. I thought that maybe keeping Lithan around might provide some of those answers…If they don't know we're on to them, then we've got a better chance of learning more. If we show our hand, then we're kind of screwed."

Ash thought about my proposal for a few moments, and then sighed in frustration.

"I don't know, Ruby; it feels like a risky move. If the entity is free, then we need to keep the castle as secure as we can."

I disagreed—I didn't think the castle would ever be truly safe, not against the entity. Knowledge would be more powerful to us right now, but I chose not to say anything. There was something else about Ash tonight that was making me feel a bit on edge. It wasn't just that he was grumpy, but more that our conversation felt like it was happening between two strangers.

"Well, I'm sure we'll get to the bottom of it all eventually," I replied, trying to reassure him.

Ash nodded. "And I suppose we'll have *Varga* to thank for that."

Whoa.

"What does that mean?" I retorted.

"Nothing. I just meant the letter was helpful, that's all. Good job he had the foresight to write it to you," Ash grumbled.

Is this about jealousy?

"Only so that I'd make Tejus read it!" I exclaimed.

"I know that," he replied shortly. "Like I said—it's a good thing."

"Okay," I replied, mildly insulted that he thought I was so stupid that I couldn't see the obvious issue he had with Varga writing me a letter.

"I'm off to bed. It's been a long day," he announced. "Here, Jenney," he added, rolling the scepter down the length of the table, "you can use this to stir a stew or something."

With that, he stormed out of the room, slamming the kitchen door shut behind him. I sank back into the chair, the wind knocked out of me.

"He's *impossible*!" I groaned at Jenney. "The letter didn't mean a thing! I don't understand why he got so worked up about it."

"I don't think it's about the letter," Jenney replied softly, looking down at the floor and not quite meeting my eyes.

"What do you mean?"

"Well...I think Ash might have some other worries. And maybe Varga is the catalyst, but really I think he's fretting about the Hazel and Tejus sentry transformation thing—it must have crossed your mind?" she asked.

"Of course it's crossed my mind! And I'm worried too...but I don't think pushing each other away is going to help matters," I replied sullenly.

"I guess he's just confused. Ash likes being in control. I'm guessing he feels pretty helpless right now, and that's not going to help his mood."

I tried to empathize with Ash's behavior, but I was

struggling. We were both going through the same stuff, and though he had the added pressure of the trials, I still didn't think that gave him the right to shut me out – that wasn't going to help either of us.

"I'm going to have it out with him," I announced. In that moment, I really felt like my mother's daughter, too fiery for my own good, too impulsive. But I didn't care.

"That's a bad idea—"

"I don't *care*. I'm going anyway. I'll see you later."

I followed Ash in storming out of the kitchen. Buoyed up with anger, I marched along the servants' quarters, belatedly realizing that I didn't know where Ash would be sleeping now. I was about to meekly return to ask Jenney when I saw light coming from beneath the door of his old bedroom.

I knocked.

"Come in," he called.

I opened the door and stood at the entrance, glaring at him with my hands on my hips.

"Ruby, I told you I was—"

"*Tired*, right." I sneered, "I got it."

"But you're not going to let me get any rest?" he prompted sarcastically.

"No! I'm not. I know what you're really upset about—it's the sentry thing, isn't it?" I demanded. Ash didn't reply. He just glared back at me, his cheeks flushing red.

"Well, I feel like crap about it too!" I cried, determined that if he wasn't going to get it off his chest, it certainly wasn't going to hold *me* back. "I'm terrified of the same thing happening to me! I can see what it's like for Hazel—she can't go anywhere near her friends, or Tejus. Their relationship is breaking apart because of it, and I couldn't bear that to happen to us. The whole thing is scary and…well, just plain *weird*, and it wouldn't be my ideal way of having a relationship. I don't want to be a sentry, and I don't want to go through the same thing that's happening to Hazel. But I love you, and I'm willing to at least *try* to overcome whatever gets thrown in our way so at least this relationship can have a chance! It's difficult enough with us being from different dimensions, and now you're a king, for crying out loud. But none of that has ever held me back, because I'm not a…*coward*, but if you're going to push me away and not even try to see if we can make the best of things, then I really don't even know why I'm even bother—"

I broke up as Ash started laughing. Before I could

respond, he stood up, crushing me in his arms. I was momentarily taken aback—still angry and upset, it took me a moment to come to my senses and hug him back.

"Do you have any idea how *crazy* in love with you I am, Shortie?" he murmured into my hair.

Oh.

I hadn't been expecting that.

"You just needed to hear me say it too, didn't you?" I asked softly.

"Yeah, I did."

His grin faded and his lips met mine, kissing me softly, taking away all the anger and frustration, and just leaving me with molten insides that only cared that his kisses never stopped.

We spent the entire evening wrapped in each other's arms – doing nothing but kissing and occasionally talking. For once, we had spent the last few moments of the evening discussing anything other than the trials and the entity— instead, about all the things that didn't really matter, that meant so much more than the things that did. We lay on his bed, my head in the crook of his arm. I was starting to fall asleep, lulled by Ash's low, murmuring voice.

"Hey," I whispered, before I became too drowsy and fell asleep. "Thanks for sending Ragnhild to the temple with us. It was really sweet of you."

"What do you mean?" Ash asked with a yawn.

"Ragnhild—you sent him because you couldn't go?" I repeated.

"No…no, I didn't."

"Oh."

Maybe I misunderstood what Ragnhild had said?

"I thought you did," I replied quietly.

When I looked up to share my concerns with Ash, he was already fast asleep. Maybe the lieutenant was another sentry that we needed to keep an eye on…

JENUS

Nymphs.

I snorted in disgust. I had just seen another one dancing through the trees in one of the courtyards of the Seraq palace. It was the third I'd seen during my exploration of Queen Trina's domain. It didn't really surprise me that she associated with such pointless, irritating creatures. Tejus and Varga had often laughed about the goings-on at the palace, but had never been explicit about their nature…just enough to whet my appetite as a young man, to make me jealous beyond all reasoning, as if I was missing out on the true wonders that Nevertide had to offer. It had been infuriating. And I had hated them both for it.

The castle had very little to offer in the way of interest. It was undoubtedly beautiful, far superior than Hellswan and some of the other royal abodes I had visited with my father, but I was interested in the darker side of Queen Trina—and so far, I had witnessed nothing but potted plants, parrots and indulgent, lavish luxuries.

There was only one room that piqued my interest.

I stood outside it, listening to the sounds of the palace, ensuring that no one found me here. I was a few doors down from what I assumed was Queen Trina's main chamber, and her office next door. The door to the room was locked, and when I tried to use True Sight to see what lay within, I'd been unable to...which meant that she'd put a barrier around it. To maintain that barrier while she was absent from the castle itself was impressive, doubly so because she was currently at the Imperial trials. I would have imagined that she would need all her powers centered and focused to overcome whatever the doddering, foolish Impartial Ministers threw her way. It made the room, and its contents, *extremely* interesting.

What are you hiding?

I would find a way into that room eventually.

Dusk had settled, and I couldn't imagine that the queen would be too far away. The best hope I had of finding out whether or not the barriers to the room had any weaknesses was to keep a close eye on it.

The door faced the main hallway that ran through the center of the palace. On the other side the wall was absent—only columns stood, opening up the view to yet another verdant courtyard. Stepping out into the cool night air, I looked around for a place to hide.

Directly facing the locked door were three large clay pots containing zest trees. Crouching low behind them, I had a clear view if anyone entered or left the room. The only flaw in my plan would be if Queen Trina or one of her imbecilic ministers were to enter the courtyard from the other side. Worse would be if I was approached by a nymph—short of running away, I would have very little control of my actions if one were to speak to me directly. I could only hope that for once, fortune would be on *my* side.

It was a while before I heard footsteps approaching. For extra precaution, I had focused my mind on accelerating the growth of the zest trees so that their leafy branches now provided more camouflage for my presence.

Shortly, Queen Trina appeared at the opposite end of the hallway, accompanied by two of her ministers.

"All went according to plan," she said. "The fools told, as I hoped they might. Has there been *any* news?"

"None, your highness," a female minister responded. "We do not understand, but perhaps the vessel failed to complete the task."

"And they have him now, at the castle?"

"Yes."

"That is inconvenient," Queen Trina hissed. "Tomorrow morning I want the healer. Don't take no for an answer."

"Yes, your highness," both ministers chorused.

"You are dismissed," she replied airily.

I watched as the queen continued along the corridor. As she approached, a small twist of amusement played at the corners of her lips.

Does she know I'm here?

I didn't make a sound as she drew closer. A second later, I put my fears to rest. The queen didn't so much as look in my direction. She stood outside the locked door, pausing for a few moments, presumably removing the barrier that she'd placed there. When finished, she sighed with contentment, and, removing a large key, she unlocked the door. To my frustration, she opened the door so it was only ajar, and slid herself inside—completely preventing me from seeing what lay within.

Curse the woman!

If I wanted to barter my way back into Hellswan, I would need more than a description of a locked door.

Dare I try to open it now?

The thought was tempting but perilous. I couldn't afford to become an unwanted guest within the Seraq kingdom. After Queen Trina had offered me a place to stay, I had started to hatch a plan—a plan that I was determined would see me return to my rightful place within Hellswan.

I tried to use True Sight again, hoping that she hadn't reinstated the border. I failed. She had instantly put it back up, which at once made the room even more tempting...but also near impossible to enter.

Or do I play the innocent?

That was a more likely alternative. I was perfectly capable of pretending that I had witnessed her go into the room, and merely wished to speak to her...perhaps divulge some of my own kingdom's secrets in return for some of hers…

Resolute, I stood up and approached the door.

I knocked once, softly. A few seconds later, Queen Trina's laughter emanated from the room within.

Is she laughing at me? I raged suddenly, believing she thought me a fool. I was about to use True Sight again to check when the door swung open.

My rage disappeared. I blinked once, twice, unable to comprehend the sight that greeted me.

Queen Trina stood before me, smiling broadly with one hand resting lightly on the frame of the door. She was completely naked but for a thick, black tar-like liquid that covered her entire body from neck to toe. It ran down in thick globules, the shiny surface catching the light of the torches in the hallway and glistening—undulating across her skin like the tar itself was alive.

What is this?

I continued to stare at her, too shocked to say a word, my plan running off into the ether as fear penetrated my body. There was something so repellent about it—the coquettish smile on her face, the dark, unnatural liquid that swarmed over her as if to consume her.

"Jenus, what a pleasant surprise," she murmured, indicating that my presence was anything *but* a surprise. "I had hoped you would visit me here. This"—she gestured to the oozing liquid—"is a gift from my master. An incredibly generous gift. It has the most miraculous healing properties. You look as if you could benefit from it—would you consider joining me?" She stood aside, revealing the interior of the room. It was completely bare, save for a large pool in the center of the room—there the repugnant black liquid bubbled and burped like some giant sprawling creature.

"Allow yourself this gift, Jenus," she whispered, turning her back to me and slowly walking back to the pool. She stepped up onto the edge of the marble rim, and then slowly lowered herself back down.

She laughed again, beckoning to me.

"Jenus, come," she purred, "there really is no need to be afraid."

Rose

We traveled as slowly as we could along the portal that led to the supernatural dimension, waiting for Nuriya to indicate where we should 'turn off' for the In-Between. I felt weightless within the misty blue walls of the tunnel, my hand clutching Caleb's as we tried to keep as close to the walls as possible.

Up ahead, Corrine, Mona, Aisha and Horatio followed Nuriya, the witch using her magic to prevent Caleb and me from being sucked downward by the vacuum. Behind us, Yuri, Claudia, Ashley and Landis followed. The jinn started to slow down, and Nuriya pointed off into the swirling mists. Corrine and Mona again assisted us with their powers, allowing us to follow the jinn's lead, and we started to pass through the walls. Blanketed by vapors, I felt like I'd stepped into a dream-like snowstorm. The nothingness of the portal wall, the complete and utter silence of the blanketing mists started to get to me. I wanted to yell out—to make *some* sort of sound—to end the deafening silence. But as we passed through to the other side, it had only just begun.

A noiseless, star-studded eternity surrounded us. I saw what looked like planets far off in the distance, glowing. We moved slowly, drifting downward. I glanced over at Caleb, smiling—we had often wondered what the In-Between would be like after hearing my brother's experiences with it. He was as amazed as I was, his brown eyes widening as he peered into the great abyss of stars.

The jinn suddenly vanished us all, and the next thing I knew, we had traveled far away from the portal and were hovering above a star. Not one of the brightly glowing ones, but a dull sphere that looked dark and gloomy and unwelcoming.

Nuriya cleared her throat, beckoning us to follow her. Without me doing anything, I felt my body changing trajectory, moving toward the jinni. Soon, all of us were gathered around her, floating gently in the air.

"Before we arrive, I need to tell you about the Shadowed. They are the creatures that guard the stones. They won't harm us, but stay out of their way as best you can," Nuriya informed us.

"Wh-What kind of creatures?" Claudia asked, taking the words right out of my mouth. Nuriya hadn't mentioned anything about 'guardians of the stones'.

"You will see," she replied.

I gulped. I didn't much like the sound of that.

"How do you know all this anyway?" Aisha grumbled, looking toward the planet with trepidation.

"My grandfather," Nuriya replied with a regal swipe of her hair, ignoring Aisha's tone. "He brought me here when I was little. The In-Between was an old, forgotten land that our people used as a dumping ground…it was a point of interest in the history of our kind."

Without warning, the jinni jolted us down to the surface of the planet—one moment we were suspended in mid-air, the next, my feet were on solid ground. Looking around, I saw that Nuriya had placed us on a large, volcanic rock that jutted out from the earth. Beneath us, and for as far as I could see in the distance, the rest of the planet was covered in dull stones, small and perfectly round replicas of the one that had shot out from the portal.

"This place is *weird*," Aisha whispered, shivering at the sudden drop of temperature. I agreed, but I didn't think that 'weird' covered it—this place was isolated and bleak. I wasn't in any hurry to spend any more time here than we absolutely had to.

"Let's collect the stones—"

I broke off as I saw Caleb pointing, his gaze fixed on an approaching figure in the distance.

"Shadowed?" he questioned Nuriya.

"Shadowed," she confirmed, nodding grimly.

The figure loped toward us. Its movements were heavy and slow, at odds with its almost ghost-like appearance. As it got closer, I saw that the creature had been drained of all its color, making it look more like a negative photo of something that had once been and now no longer was. The most shocking thing, the part I hadn't expected, was that the figure looked like it had once been human, or close to it. Yet it couldn't be an actual ghost, for we could see it.

The jaw of the Shadowed hung open, its gaping mouth nothing but a black hole from which a low, guttural moan emerged. Catching sight of us, but unable to reach the top of the rock from where it stood, the Shadowed started to roar, its expression growing confused and angry.

"Shadowed!" Nuriya called down to it. "We mean no harm—we pledge to protect the integrity of the stones. Leave us."

The creature abruptly stopped groaning, its jaw now hanging slack and useless. Its shoulders hunched over, and it slowly turned around, moving back the way it had come.

My first reaction to the Shadowed was revulsion, but now it was pity.

"Those things remind me of the mindless humans at Murckbeech," I muttered with a shiver. "What are they anyway—or *were* they?"

"You won't like the answer," Nuriya replied sharply. Her pillowy lips pursed. "It is best left unsaid."

"Nuriya," Claudia and Corrine pressed.

The jinni sighed, taking out the felt bag that she had brought along for the stones. She handed it to Aisha, and the younger girl opened it up dutifully. I waited for Nuriya to continue, knowing that the woman, being jinn royalty, didn't take kindly to being prompted.

Impatient, I took out the gloves that we'd all packed for

the stone collecting. If one stone could have the bizarre effect it had on Corrine, then I didn't want to take any chances when we were faced with an entire planet of them.

I spied more Shadowed approaching in the distance. They didn't seem to be in any hurry to reach us, as they watched us from afar with their silent, open jaws. It gave me the creeps.

"The fae created the Shadowed," Nuriya replied eventually. "The story goes that when the fae heard of the jinn dumping stones in the In-Between, they panicked. It was impossible to remove them all, so the fae used this planet as a punishment for their people…any fae banished from one of their four planets was sent here. They soon realized that the fae who remained on this planet had their minds addled—the stones took their effect, sending the banished fae into madness."

"That's barbaric," I breathed. "How could the fae do this?"

"The fae can be cruel," Nuriya replied with a shrug. "I don't pretend to understand their ways."

We all looked at one another. I supposed we already knew very well that fae could be ruthless—going by what Sherus and his comrades had done to my brother, hoodwinking and kidnapping him to The Underworld along with countless poor disembodied souls.

"We need to have a word with Sherus," I concluded. "The Shadowed should be removed from this land. It's horrible."

"I couldn't agree more," Mona replied, shaking her head. "We should at least give them the chance to try to be healed. I don't know if they're too far gone, but maybe with fae powers...I don't know."

"I think this is enough," Nuriya interrupted, holding up a bag filled to the brim with the dull stones.

I nodded, adding a few more that I'd just picked up.

"Let's go," I replied.

As Nuriya jolted us back up into the starry galaxy, I vowed that we would speak to Sherus soon. If we were helping the fae with their request, then they needed to be mindful of the fact that the whole reason for GASP's existence was the protection of those within the supernatural and human worlds—this included the mysterious world of the "In-Between". Barbaric treatment of undesirables would not be tolerated... My father was not going to be pleased when he heard about this.

Ash

I left Ruby fast asleep in the cramped single bed that we'd shared. I dressed quickly, careful not to wake her. I wondered how long it had been since she'd had an uninterrupted sleep without being plagued by the worries of where her friends were, if they were safe or if *she* was safe. The danger was far from over; if the entity was free to rise, then none of us knew what the next few days would bring—but at least for the moment, she could rest knowing that everyone she loved was alive.

Leaving the room, I shut the door quietly behind me and went to the kitchen to grab something to eat before I left for the Fells. I wanted to get there early, hopefully without the ministers joining me, and see if I could speak to Memenion before the trials began. If he was as determined to bring down Queen Trina as I was, then perhaps we could come up with a plan. If the Acolytes were the worshipers of the entity, then once it had risen, I didn't know where that might leave the queen—by then she might be untouchable.

The kitchen was bare except for a basket of bread on the table. I walked over and took what I could carry. I was starting to feel the effects of being unable to syphon off Ruby before the trials, and food was the only option I had for keeping up my energy levels.

"Hey." Ruby's sleepy voice came from the door.

"Why are you up?" I asked. "You need to go back to sleep—it's hardly dawn yet." Her hair was mussed, and I could see slight creases on her cheeks from where she'd lain on the blankets.

"I wanted to wish you good luck." She smiled, yawning. "Can I get you anything?" Ruby looked around the kitchen, frowning slightly as she saw how empty it was— and belatedly realizing she wouldn't know *how* to get me anything.

"I don't need anything, Shortie." I grinned and held up the bread, noticing the quick flash of relief on her face.

Moved by the fact that she'd bothered to get up and wish me well, I suddenly had an overwhelming urge to gather her up in my arms and return to my room—but I knew where that would lead, and as much as I wished I could spend the day ignoring the rest of the world with her, it just wasn't possible.

"I'll see you later." I walked up to her, kissing her briefly on the forehead.

"Wait, Ash." She hesitated briefly. "I just wanted to say that we'll find a way—to be together, I mean. Whatever happens."

I tugged at a strand of her blonde hair, wanting to say so much more than I was about to. "You can count on it, Shortie," I replied. "I'm not letting you go anywhere."

She smiled up at me. "Okay. Deal."

We shared a brief hug, and then I made my way to the courtyard, still hoping that neither Lithan or Qentos would be ready yet.

My heart sank as I opened the side door of the castle and saw Lithan up ahead, cooing to a vulture. My blood boiled as I surveyed him.

Treacherous coward.

How dare he even show his face here? When I thought about how long he must have been playing a double game, throughout the emperor's rule, through the kingship trials and now the Imperial trials...It made me sick.

I thought about what Ruby had said, about trying to keep the monster on our side, and tried to still my temper before it got the better of me.

Attempting to appear normal, I approached the courtyard. My feet crunched loudly on gravel, and the minister turned. As soon as he recognized his intruder, a look of fury flickered across his expression before he reverted it to a mask of polite indifference.

"You're up early, your highness," he announced in greeting.

"As are you," I replied.

"I wanted to ensure all was ready."

I nodded, not believing the sentry for a second.

"And where is Qentos?" I asked.

"Already at the pavilion. I believe he wished to discuss a matter with the Impartial Ministers."

Interesting.

I wondered if Qentos was just as embroiled in the

Acolytes as Lithan was. Qentos had always seemed the lesser of two evils, but maybe that was just a ruse.

"Take this bird, your highness," Lithan continued, standing back from the vulture. "One of the stable hands is bringing me another."

"I can wait," I replied. I didn't want to fly on a bird that Lithan had been whispering to for however long.

"It's no trouble," he insisted. I didn't know if it was my imagination or not, but I thought I could detect the gleam of malice in his eyes. Now I was in a tricky situation. If I protested again, I risked Lithan thinking I didn't trust him...but if I didn't, I questioned my chances of getting to the trials in one piece.

As quickly as I could, I called to Tejus's bird. I didn't know if it would respond to me—his previous one had been exclusively loyal to her master, but it was the only bird that I knew I could trust. The only one Lithan and Qentos wouldn't dare go near.

"Please, your highness." Lithan bowed deeply, gesturing to the creature.

I was about to come up with some meaningless reason to return back to the castle for a moment when a loud squawk and heavy flap of wings broke through the stillness of the morning.

"Tejus's vulture?" Lithan questioned as he looked to the sky, his tone clipped.

"Tejus's vulture," I repeated. "The ex-king has been very accommodating."

"So I see." Lithan nodded, a venomous smile erupting across his features. "Very well then, we shall depart."

The vulture settled on the stones of the courtyard, waiting patiently for me to climb onto its back. I grinned back at Lithan.

"Let's go."

* * *

We set down a few yards from the pavilion. We were the first to arrive—the ghostly white of the crumbling structure was only just beginning to be soaked in the morning light, making it look even more ancient and decrepit than usual.

"I can't see Qentos," I commented, feeling vaguely uneasy that I was alone in the Fells with Lithan. If Queen Trina arrived early too, then I would be surrounded by the enemy.

"Perhaps he is on his way here with the Impartial

Ministers." Lithan shrugged. "I am not his keeper."

I resisted the urge to snap at him, and instead petted the neck of the vulture, beyond grateful that I had not been left at Lithan's mercy.

"Queen Trina arrives." Lithan delivered the news with glee, looking off into the distance behind me. I spun around. Sure enough, I could see the distinct formation of three birds of prey soaring through the sky toward us.

This doesn't look good.

Would Queen Trina dare to harm me before the trials had even begun? I realized, with a sinking feeling, that she would.

I buried my hand in the feathers of the bird. If I needed to make a quick escape, I could. There would be no bravery in trying to battle Queen Trina with only her cohorts around me. I had seen what she had done to Hadalix, and most likely Varga…I didn't want to end up the same way.

"I wish you to locate Qentos," I improvised. "He has something I need."

"Now?" Lithan retorted. "The trials will commence shortly—I tell you, he is with the Impartial Ministers."

"Now—and that's a command, Lithan."

I stared the minister down, noting with satisfaction the blood rising to his cheeks at the shame of receiving a direct order from the 'kitchen boy'. He grunted, jumping up onto his vulture.

He slammed his heels into the bird viciously, and it squawked in pain, but flapped up into the air as it had been commanded. Lithan's teeth were clenched with barely concealed frustration, and with one last, lingering look at Queen Trina's approaching entourage, he flew off in the direction of the forest.

The second he departed, I heard the sharp pounding of hooves emerging from the western point of the pavilion. Using True Sight, I saw Memenion approach with his ministers, his gaze fixed up in the sky while he spurred the heard of bull-horses and their riders onward, evidently not wanting the queen to outrun him. The king could obviously see that I would be left at her mercy were she to arrive first, and as he sped on his horse, any reservations I still had as to whether I could trust Memenion or not disappeared.

Queen Trina landed, but only a few seconds before Memenion emerged from the thickets of the forest, his bull-horse grunting from the exertion. Trina scowled, disembarking from her bird as she looked warily from me to the approaching king. I grinned at her.

Better luck next time.

She turned away in disgust, speaking in hissed whispers to her ministers.

I walked swiftly toward the pavilion, hoping to have a word with Memenion before others arrived. The king caught up with me as I entered the dome of the structure, and, nimbly ascending the steps, he greeted me with a warm smile.

"That was a close call," he said.

"I can't thank you enough—I thought it might be my body tied to the arches this time," I replied with grateful relief.

"Any news? How's Tejus?" the king asked, solemnity returning.

"He believes the entity is now released. The stones from the castle have been taken to the temple of the Acolytes, and the human boy, Benedict, doesn't seem to be under possession any longer…"

"But there have been no further signs?" the king deduced.

"None. Not that we know of, anyway."

The king nodded.

"Then we wait," he replied.

I nodded. I also needed to tell him about Varga's letter, but I wondered if its contents should wait till after the trial. If Memenion knew about his son being a member of the Acolytes, he would no doubt be devastated, potentially distracting him from whatever the Impartial Ministers had in store for us. But he had a right to know.

"Spit it out, boy," Memenion commanded, observing my hesitation.

"Varga's letter," I replied, looking around us to make sure that there wasn't a soul who could overhear.

"Ah, I did wonder what that would contain. We found it tucked beneath the saddle of his bull-horse—the creature was wandering the Fells in a sorry state. Was there anything helpful?"

I nodded, hating what I was about to do.

"Varga was, in the past, a member of the Acolytes." I paused as Memenion's face drained of all color, but the king allowed me to continue without interruption. "He was silenced by their threats, and never told Tejus or anyone outside the cult what he was. In his letter, he divulged two members he knew were active. One was

Lithan—"

"The swine!" Memenion bellowed. "He should be hanged for his disloyalty—though it comes as no real surprise. He was always a master manipulator, and I warned Tejus of this."

"The second…the second was your son, Ronojoy."

I stared at the floor, not wanting to see Memenion's grief. A long silence passed. I could hear the movement of the evergreens in the breeze, and the cooing of birds back where Queen Trina and her entourage were standing. When I looked back up at Memenion's face, he looked like he had aged a hundred years.

"It is my own fault," the king whispered. "I should have known. I believed Ronojoy to be discontented, but I didn't take the time to ask why—or take an interest in his life beyond him being taught in a manner which I thought was appropriate. I abandoned him. His faults lie with me."

"It's not your fault," I replied earnestly. "The Acolytes turned Varga—I know he was your friend. They are obviously able to be…*tempting*."

The king shook his head.

"I was a bad father, and I know it. Don't try to alleviate my blame, Ashbik. It is mine to suffer."

I realized that I wouldn't be able to say anything that would make this better for him, and that the kindest, most honorable thing I could do was remain silent and allow Memenion to grieve. I just couldn't get my head around the fact that the king could have a son who would turn to something like the Acolytes. How had the boy not wanted to grow up in the footsteps of his father?

Before I could say another word, the Impartial Ministers appeared at the edge of the grassland. Lithan was among them. I scanned the group for Qentos, but I couldn't see him. Perhaps Lithan had purposefully left him behind at the castle, but I didn't have time to question the snake—the trials were about to begin.

BENEDICT

It took me a moment to work out where I was. I had been
expecting to see the rune-covered walls of the temple and
the eerie green glow that seemed to constantly seep out of
its walls, no matter what time of day it was…but when I
first opened my eyes, I could see gray walls and light
streaming through a window.

Yelena.

She was sitting on the opposite bed, a cushion clutched
to her stomach and her red hair looking like it was on fire
as it caught the light.

"Benedict?" She called my name softly, staring over at

me, and I noticed how dark the shadows were under her eyes—she looked even smaller than I remembered her. Still, I didn't think I could remember ever being so pleased to see anyone in my life. If she was here, it meant that I was in the castle, I was safe, at least for now, and most importantly, I hadn't done anything to seriously harm her.

"Hey," I croaked. My throat felt like sandpaper. "How did I get here?"

The last thing I could remember was being in the temple, talking to Hazel and Ruby through the wall...and Julian? Had Julian been there? I couldn't work out if it was wishful thinking or not.

"You collapsed at the cove—when the entity left you, apparently."

I'm free?

"Was Julian there?" I asked.

"He was." She nodded. "Queen Trina had him in a dungeon, and then Ruby was put there too, and Ash went to rescue her...only to find them both!"

I gulped.

"So Queen Trina is bad news?" I asked, thinking that I'd been a massive idiot to trust her at all.

"*Really* bad news," Yelena confirmed.

I sank back into the pillows. I was glad that Julian was safe, but hearing that Queen Trina had something to do with it drove me crazy. If I'd told Hazel earlier about all this, then Julian never would have been imprisoned—or at least he would have been rescued earlier.

"So what's happening now?" I asked. "Those stones…how much damage did I do?"

Yelena's face fell a fraction, and I braced myself for bad news. I had known all along that those stones were dangerous. I shouldn't have been going anywhere near them, but I had felt powerless to stop myself. Every morning I'd wake up in the temple, only having vague flashes of images from the night before. I would find more stones dancing in the grooves on the table, and I knew that I'd somehow collected more of them in the night.

"It's not your fault, Benedict—you weren't in control."

"Just tell me," I replied. "I need to know. And I'd rather hear it from you than anyone else."

She twisted a strand of her hair, uncomfortable with my searching gaze. I sighed. I wasn't so sure I liked it when Yelena pitied me, as she so clearly did now. It was better when we were arguing and she could happily tell me to go to hell without treating me like I was some poor invalid that she had to protect.

"Yelena," I prompted, irritated with her silence.

"Okay. But don't go blaming yourself for any of it. It's the entity, not you. And the stupid queen, and the acolytes. *And* the stupid ministers."

"Yeah, sure," I agreed dryly, "everyone's fault but mine."

"Do you want some water?" she asked brightly.

I rolled my eyes, and picked up the full glass that had been left by my bedside.

"I'm good—get on with it."

She mumbled something under her breath that I couldn't hear, and then started to tell me what had happened since the night I left Hellswan. She jumped off the bed, pacing up and down the small room as she spoke, gesticulating wildly and occasionally going off on rants about Trina and the ministers—even the rest of the kids in the living quarters weren't immune to her scorn.

"Ash is king?" I interrupted when she mentioned he was at the Imperial trials.

"Oh, yeah—he's king."

"What about Tejus?" I asked, stunned.

She waved her arms around. "Oh, he got wounded in a

trial, I think, and then decided to do the honorable thing—honestly, I think it was to impress your sister anyway."

That made no sense whatsoever, but I chose to ignore it—I could ask Hazel about that later.

"But everyone's safe for the time being?" I asked.

"For the time being, yeah. Everyone's happy you're back—though maybe you need to be careful walking around. You kind of syphoned off a lot of ministers and guards...I think they're a bit afraid of you."

I digested the information. It didn't actually bother me that much...

"But you're not, right?"

"Afraid of you?" she scoffed. "No!"

"Good," I replied curtly.

Her face reddened a bit, and I knew that she was holding back on me. I could remember flashes of Yelena lying down on the floor, looking almost dead with her face as white as a ghost's. Of her screaming, crying out for me to stop—and me *not* stopping.

"I'm so sorry," I murmured. "I didn't—"

"How many times do I need to tell you? I *know* you didn't do it!"

She was starting to get angry now, so I kept my mouth shut, feeling sick with guilt. Maybe there would be some way I could repay her…but I doubted it. It wasn't like I could protect her from the entity when it finally rose—I'd had the thing inside my head and still didn't know anything about it, or what it actually wanted beyond the stones.

"Where is everyone, anyway?" I asked, changing the subject.

"I don't know." Yelena shrugged. "Hazel's probably still sleeping—she's had it rough the past couple of days."

"What do you mean?" I asked sharply. She hadn't mentioned my sister being in any danger.

Yelena visibly winced.

"What?" I snapped at her.

She took a deep breath, and then mumbled something under her breath, sounding like, 'blah, blah, sentry, blah'.

"Yelena—*what?*"

"I said," she yelled, "your sister's a sentry now!"

"A what?" I replied, wondering if I'd just gone deaf, because it sounded like Yelena had just told me that my sister was a sentry.

"Oh, my God—you heard me. She's a sentry, and she's

having a really difficult time controlling her powers...and keeps syphoning off everyone by accident. Tejus can handle it a bit, but the rest of us can't—she is *super* strong."

"Did Tejus do this to her?" I asked, still not really understanding what the hell had happened—how in the world could Hazel become one of *them*?

"Umm...sort of, by mistake though," she added hurriedly.

"How?"

Yelena's cheeks went crimson and she snickered, avoiding meeting my eyes.

"What? I don't....oh."

Oh.

Eugh.

It must be a stupid love thing.

"Don't even tell me—GROSS!" I exploded.

How could she?

Yelena laughed at me, but her blush intensified.

"They're in love, stupid. I wish a man like Tejus would love *me* that much," she replied dreamily.

I snorted with derision.

Whatever.

Yelena could be such an idiot sometimes.

ROSE

We emerged from the portal onto the snowy whiteness of Mount Logan. Nuriya clutched the bag of stones tightly to her chest, looking sidelong at Corrine.

"I'm not going to touch them," the witch mumbled.

"Make sure you don't," the jinni replied. "None of you—until we're doing the spell."

"I don't want to lose time," I sighed, knowing that my dad needed to be told about the Shadowed. I didn't want him putting his or anyone else's lives in danger for the fae if they were behaving in such diabolical ways.

"Let me go and speak to the council," Caleb replied.

281

"You don't need me for the spell. I'll make it back as soon as the portal is opened—just let me know and I'll get one of the witches to transport me."

"That would be great," I said. "Hopefully it won't take long."

"It will take as long as it takes," Nuriya interjected. "Don't hope for a quick miracle—that portal is ancient, and I'm not sure this is even going to work."

"I know," I replied quickly. "But I'm still hopeful. It's the only chance we have right now…it's got to work."

"Let's get back to the rest of the group," Corrine asserted. "They're going to be wondering what the holdup is."

"Okay," I said, glancing at my husband. "Will you take Caleb back and then we can all go together?"

Corrine nodded.

"Be careful," Caleb said, clutching my hands. He knew I could be as reckless as he could, especially when it came to protecting someone I loved.

I nodded and kissed his lips. Then in the next moment, both he and the witch were gone.

I'll find us a way in, Caleb. I fiercely made the silent promise to my husband. I knew that the whole of GASP was behind us, but when it came down to it, our kids were in that portal, and I wouldn't rest until Caleb and I were in whatever alternate dimension was hidden behind that black goo—whether the stones worked or not.

A few moments later Corrine reappeared.

Horatio, Aisha and Nuriya all agreed to join us on the trip back to Fair Isle. I was glad that the jinn would be joining us—if the stones had been created by their people, however long ago, then it made sense to me that their magic would be more attuned to them.

Corrine transported us all back to the door of the moldy pub where the others waited. One of the witches, Shayla, rushed out to greet us, shielding us all from the downpours of rain that were currently drenching the small island.

We hurried inside, greeting the small army of witches and vamps who were ready to do whatever it took to get the portal open. It was a reassuring sight.

"Did you get what you need?" Shayla asked.

"We did."

I decided not to immediately divulge the information on the Shadowed. It was something that could wait until we'd opened up the portal; Dad would now be the one to decide what would happen there—and work it out with

Sherus.

"We should get going." I looked to Corrine and Mona, who both nodded.

"There's a storm coming," Mona replied. "I can hold the worst of it off, but not without diverting my energy from the portal, so the sooner we get going, the better."

"Hold hands, everyone," Corrine instructed, "and don't let go once we arrive at the portal. I want our power at its strongest."

In an instant, we were out in the middle of the ocean— fierce waves spraying us with salt water as we hovered in a circle around the black mass of tar. The wind whipped at my hair, taking it out of its clasp so I could hardly see what was going on around me. Corrine tightened her grip on my hand, as if reminding me not to let go.

Suddenly, the bag of stones shot out into the middle of the circle. One by one, the dull-colored pebbles emerged and started to form a circular shape which hovered just above the mouth of the portal.

While the storm raged on around us, I noticed that we were immune to the worst of it—Mona had obviously decided to use some of her powers to protect us, but I wished she hadn't. I wanted all her focus on the stones, but I also knew it certainly wasn't my place to tell the witch what to do.

So I waited.

I glanced over at Claudia, who had the same hopeful and fierce expression on her face that I imagined I had on mine—we were both determined that this would work. No one said a word as the witches and jinn all focused on the small stones floating in front of us.

Please work, I prayed silently.

Even though I knew I couldn't make any difference of my own, I willed the stones to work their magic—copying the witches' intense focus, not removing my glare from their smooth surface. I did worry for a moment that we were working with objects that contained malevolent, ancient creatures, but recalling Nuriya's words reassured me. We weren't powerful enough to open them – whatever was contained within would stay there while we borrowed their energy…I just hoped it was enough.

Corrine inhaled sharply next to me, and in that moment, one of the stones started to glow. It was only faint at first, a slight luminosity appearing in a green haze around it, but before long the others started to do the same—each stone glowing a slightly different hue till all the stones made up every color of the rainbow.

Oh, my… It's working!

BEN

"Is that all we have?" my father asked wearily.

I nodded with the same fed-up expression. We had been researching for days, but hadn't come up with anything that might even hint at a supernatural power emerging somewhere on Earth. The only stand-out event had been a hurricane, but it all appeared perfectly normal—it had started in the Atlantic Ocean, drifting over to Miami, and hadn't caused any great devastation other than a few fallen trees and some miserable holiday-goers.

"Is there nothing further you can tell us, nothing at all?" my father asked Sherus for what felt like the millionth time.

The fae shook his head. "I wish I could, but I have nothing more to go on. I had hoped that more would reveal itself, perhaps even in a dream, but there has been nothing."

I tried to hide my irritation. I believed the fae that something was headed our way, but right now we also had family members stuck in another dimension that we knew nothing about, and I felt like both mine and Dad's efforts would be of better use helping Rose and Caleb and the rest of the witches.

"I don't have much," my mom said as she entered the room, holding some printed papers aloft. "A slight rise in Assault and Battery charges, street arrests slightly higher, and a spike in young people being sectioned under the Mental Health Act in coastal areas, which I actually thought might be of interest to Rose…it reminded me of those Murkbeech children."

"We should inform her," my father agreed. "But I think right now they're at the portal, and nothing else sounds like it's going to be helpful to us."

"No." My mother shook her head. "It's pretty quiet all over the world."

"What portal?" Lidera asked sharply.

I glanced at her, belatedly realizing that we had filled Sherus in on the situation with the GASP kids, but not his sister.

"We have reason to believe that some of the kids who were sent off to a summer camp have been taken into another dimension—there's a portal in the North Atlantic that they're investigating. It's locked, but jinn have been called in to assist the witches in opening it." I gave her the shortened version of the story, hoping that we could skip past it and get the meeting tied up—if there was any way we could help Mona and Corrine get it open, I wanted in.

Lidera's eyes narrowed as soon as the jinn were mentioned.

"Doesn't this portal sound like it could have something to do with the signs Sherus is experiencing? Do we even know what's contained within it, where it leads?" she asked.

"Perhaps," I replied. "We'll know soon enough, they've spent all day trying to open it."

Before I could say another word, Caleb entered the room, his usually controlled appearance transformed into agitation as he stalked in, frowning at the two fae.

"Derek, Ben—I need to speak to you," he announced, his brown gaze still fixed on Sherus and Lidera in deep disdain.

"Go ahead, Caleb," my father replied, looking curiously at his son-in-law.

"The jinn took us to the In-Between, to visit a planet containing stones that we needed to access the portal. When we arrived, we came face to face with creatures that the jinn call the Shadowed—fae who live out their lives on the planet as punishment, being slowly driven insane by the power of the stones. They have become pitiful wretches of the creatures they once were." He turned once more and glared at Sherus. "It is inhumane, an abomination. We cannot help those who hold their own people's lives in such disregard."

My father and I turned to Sherus in stunned silence. Was this true?

I expected the fae to deny it, but instead he rose from his seat with a look of horror on his face.

"What makes you think that the stones will open the portal?" he asked in a whisper.

"So you do not deny it?" Caleb retorted.

"Tell me about the stones," the king insisted, ignoring

Caleb's accusations.

"One emerged from the portal. One of the jinn said she recognized it, and that more of them might hold enough power to overcome whatever bound it shut," Caleb replied, his temper draining in the face of Sherus's ambivalence to the charges being laid at his door.

"And you are opening the portal now, with these stones?"

"Yes."

Caleb's reply was terse, but I knew him well enough to know that he was starting to question their actions.

"You FOOL!" Sherus slammed his fist down on the table in anger. "The jinn used those stones to lock in the most evil and dark souls. The In-Between became a dumping ground for jinn undesirables—and you have just opened a portal using the very same stones? You have no idea what might be contained within that dimension! No idea of the horror that might be unleashed! It could be full of the creatures that the jinn held bound—and held bound with good reason!"

"Has the portal been opened yet?" my father asked quickly.

"No, not yet," Caleb said.

"Then stop it at once!" Sherus roared.

"Our KIDS are in there!" Caleb replied, his fangs shooting out as he hissed at the fae king. "That portal needs to be opened!"

"Get Rose on the phone," my father commanded. "Before it's too late."

ASH

The Impartial Ministers stepped up onto the pavilion. For the first time since I was a young boy, their appearance didn't stir in me the same reverence and respect that I'd always held them in. Now they seemed as crooked as Lithan, no more mysterious and worldly than the ministers who worked for the Hellswan kingdom…and I had always held them in complete contempt. Jenney and I had spent many long hours in the kitchen discussing their misdeeds—the mistresses, the drunkenness and the narrow-minded attitude of most of them had always reduced us to tears of laughter. Now the idiocy of both the ministers and the Impartial Ministers no longer seemed like a joke, but a deadly mistake. How had the kingdoms continued to let them wield so much power? How had we all been so blind to their limitations?

One of them banged down a wooden staff, designed to command immediate attention. Memenion's and Queen Trina's ministers stood to attention immediately, but Memenion barely glanced in their direction—no doubt still fixated on the news I'd just delivered. I knew it had been a mistake to tell him prior to the trial. If anything were to happen to him, I would only have myself to blame.

"We have come to the penultimate trial. Those of you who have gotten this far, congratulate yourselves on your fortitude and know that it will stand you in good stead as you continue to rule your kingdoms."

I wanted to laugh. What about the kingdoms that had lost perfectly good leaders because of these trials? Hadalix, Thraxus—both good kings who would be missed by their people. It suddenly seemed like a meaningless waste...lives lost because of the games of a few old, decrepit men.

"The trial will be a test of your willpower to see if you can resist the strongest call—that of the heart's desire. To see if you can put lust and desire aside to do the honorable thing—to answer to integrity, to faith."

I resisted the urge to scoff. The Ministers didn't know anything about integrity or honor. If they did, they wouldn't be standing here, preaching to us as Nevertide sank further and further into its inevitable end. Why were we standing around a stone pavilion, being tested, while the entity rose?

"No weapons will be needed for the trial," the minister began. "You are the only weapon that will—"

The Minister broke off suddenly as the ground beneath the pavilion started to rumble with a low, insistent tremor. After a few moments, it stopped.

"As I was saying, you alone will be the weapon—"

A resounding crack splintered the air. It was a few moments before I realized that the sound had come from the stone of the pavilion—a split ran through the center, a jagged hairline that divided the stone in two. The split widened, dust pluming up from the stone and the black crevice yawning open.

Everyone staggered back, holding on to the arches as the rumbles from the earth began again, sending the ornate decorations at the top of the arches crashing to the floor and smashing into thousands of pieces. I looked around, noticing that the disturbance wasn't isolated to the pavilion. All around us the trees were starting to shake. Horrific tearing sounds screamed from the depths of the forest—the screeches of rock cracking and grinding against itself, and then the low rumble of timber whistling through the air as the trees began to collapse.

"What is going on?" one of the ministers roared, slamming his staff down as if he could command nature itself to stop and obey him.

All around us, the ground was starting to split open. The cracks ran across the earth as if nature itself was dividing up the six kingdoms, severing our lands. Rocks leered up from the depths of the soil, jutting off at odd angles, their stone as black as night and jagged.

I heard the cries of the birds; they had all launched themselves up into the sky, too terrified to land, and had begun to circle the chaos beneath. As I looked up, I stumbled backward instinctively—the sky had torn.

That makes no sense!

But it was the only logical explanation for what I could see. The morning sky, gold and pink, had been carelessly ripped open, leaving a long, ragged scar that revealed the night's sky—an endless black dotted with the cold glow of stars.

What in Nevertide is happening?

I watched, astonished, as one of the arches of the pavilion launched itself forward. As if in slow motion, the stone came toppling down, its already broken tip spearing the body of one of the Ministers who hadn't thought to move in time—had thought that he was immune to the dangers that ravaged the land around us. His body crumpled to the floor.

As if some switch had been flicked inside me, I immediately came to my senses—I needed to run.

"MEMENION!" I bellowed over the noise, catching his attention as he stumbled back from the steps of the pavilion. Righting himself, he ran forward, his ministers behind him. Launching himself over the gaping crevice in the stone, he landed a meter away from me, skidding to a halt.

I pointed up at the birds, indicating that we needed one of them to land. Simultaneously we started to run for the forest edge back where I'd originally landed. The black rocks created an obstacle course, but the earth's cracks were smaller. If we reached the edge of the forest and managed to get one of the birds to land, we might have a chance. I turned to look behind me once, relived to see that Memenion was keeping pace—but Queen Trina had the same idea, and was hot on our heels.

I launched myself forward, feeling another tremor erupting beneath me. I heard the creak and groan as the ground split. I heard the strangled cry as Memenion stumbled.

No!

I spun back around, diving forward to catch the king before his body was swallowed by the earth. I grabbed him around the upper torso, but he slipped further from my grasp as another tremor shook the rock. I was left with only my hand clasped onto his arm, doggedly holding on as the king looked up at me, his legs swinging above a bottomless eternity.

"Hold on!" I yelled, tightening my grip with all the strength I had. "I'm going to create a barrier!"

I wanted to look away. I saw the look of defeat in the king's eyes—he couldn't hold on for much longer.

How can I do this if you can't believe you can do this?

I wanted to scream at the king, but focused my energy on trying to secure a barrier that would hold him. On the fourth attempt, Memenion's arm slipped further.

"Help me!" I cried down to him. The barrier was impossible to secure—the earth kept shifting, breaking any bonds I tried to make, the screams of the earth shattering my concentration each time that it jolted.

Giving up, I forgot trying to create a barrier and tried to focus on catching the attention of one of the birds. I could hardly distinguish one from another, their hysteria melding them together as one as they flapped and shrieked above us in the sky. I glanced upward as I heard one of them swooping down toward Queen Trina. She was on the opposite side of the crevice. She reached her arms upward, jumping up to close the space between them and clasping the bird's claws. It rose back upward, the queen dangling from its feet. Envy shifted to shock as the bird was knocked sideways by a rock tearing upward from the ground as the creature tried to ascend. It screeched, and Queen Trina was flung onto the earth next to me, unconscious. The bird flew off.

"I'll get us another," I cried desperately to Memenion, more to reassure myself than him. I felt my grasp on the king slip once again.

"Ashbik."

I looked directly at the king, showing him that I was

listening, but not daring to speak.

"This is the work of the entity." The king spoke softly, calmly. "My son is one who set this in motion. The fault is mine. Perhaps this is the best way."

"No! No, it is not the best way. Nevertide needs you, Memenion—*I need you!*" As the words left my mouth, I realized how true they were. How would I deal with all that was to come without him? I had no one to turn to, no one who could guide me if he was gone. I couldn't do it alone. I *wouldn't.*

"HOLD ON!" I shouted down to him, determined that I wouldn't lose him.

"This is too good an end for her," he breathed, glancing in the direction of Queen Trina. "She needs to be brought to justice. Take her back with you."

"And you," I argued, as Memenion released his hand from my arm. Without the extra grip, his robe slid through my fingertips. Memenion fell through the air, his hand reaching out to mine in a silent, final salute.

Memenion.

Another crash of rock ricocheted nearby, and I scrambled to my feet. Grabbing the dead weight of Queen Trina, I lifted her over my shoulder like a sack of grain and tore off toward the trees. I focused on reaching out to Tejus's bird. I had thought that the vultures seemed like a hysterical mass, but perhaps it was the other way around.

I kept running, trying to glance in all directions as I scanned the ever-moving land for the bird. Just before I reached the trees, I heard a familiar squawk. My heart leapt as a large shadow loomed behind me. A second later, talons wrapped themselves around my waist, lifting both me and Queen Trina up in the air.

I wished dearly that it was Memenion's body I held instead of the queen's. There was no value in her life, and so much in his. The fact that he was buried at the earth's core while Trina remained above it made my blood boil.

She would suffer for this.

For every day that she lived while he didn't, she would suffer.

Hazel

I was standing on the top of Tejus's tower. The morning air was cold, and I shivered despite the two robes I'd taken from my room and wrapped around myself. The tower was the only place that I couldn't be tempted; by Tejus, by my friends, even my brother. I didn't dare see Benedict till I had this at least partway under control—right now, it had to be enough just knowing he was safe.

But I was lonely.

I'd never thought what it would be like not to touch people. Why would I? But it was only now that I realized how important it was to have human contact—a friend's hand, a nudge, a hug. It made all the difference. To be constantly conscious of avoiding brushing against people or getting too close made me feel like I was watching life unfold through a window. I didn't want every kiss between Tejus and me to end with him in pain, with him weakened. It was the exact *opposite* of what I wanted. Love should offer you strength, give you a reason to fight harder, to keep going when the odds were against you.

"What are you doing up here?"

Tejus's voice echoed from the doorway of the tower, and I jumped slightly. The morning silence had been like a blanket muffling the entirety of Hellswan, and I'd been completely lost in it.

"Avoiding people," I replied ruefully.

I heard him ascending the short steps up to the top of the parapet and turned to face him. I was relieved to see some color in his cheeks for the first time in a while—he had obviously slept well, and although the gaunt, hungry look hadn't left his face (and I doubted that it ever really would), he didn't seem to be suffering from my syphoning last night...

"Did you sleep in my emerald room?" I asked curiously. When I'd first arrived in Hellswan, Tejus had made me sleep in his small cubby hole of a room containing energy crystals that were intended to sharpen my mind.

"I didn't sleep there, no. But I did visit."

"No, of course not—wouldn't catch *you* sleeping in there, right?" I mocked.

He came to stand beside me, both of us turning to look out onto the kingdom. I moved over a bit, making sure I kept an arm's length distance between us.

"I'm glad you're here though." I smiled.

"I often choose to avoid people, though for very different reasons," he muttered.

"You surprise me,"I replied, rolling my eyes.

His reply made me smile despite myself. It was so typical of Tejus—his taciturn nature had gotten us into this stupid situation to begin with, but it also always drew me to him. It made me want to know what it was that he held back, having to rely on my instincts to know what he was feeling, having to learn to be honest enough for the both of us.

"I wanted you to have this," he continued, taking an object from his belt and holding it out in front of me. It was a dagger – the blade sheathed, with a beautiful, ornately carved, golden handle that resembled a serpent.

The pommel had been made to look like the serpent's mouth – between its curved fangs, a brilliant ice-blue stone was held in its mouth. It looked as if a white light was emanating from the stone's very center, clearer and more bright than anything I'd ever seen.

Cautiously, careful not to touch him, I raised my hand to take the dagger by the handle.

"It's beautiful," I breathed. "What is it?"

"A mercy dagger. It belonged to my mother."

I handed it back to him quickly.

"I can't, Tejus—"

"You can. Please—I want you to have it."

He pushed the dagger toward me again, and this time I took it. It was heavier than I expected, and up close, more beautiful. I removed the blade from its sheath, marveling at its elegant curvature – a subtle 's' shape that seemed strangely feminine.

"It's not from a lock, is it?" I joked lamely, referring to the stone in the pommel, feeling awkward at the magnitude of the gift.

"No."

"Thank you," I replied hesitantly. "You said it was a mercy dagger…what does that mean?"

I had never heard of such an instrument, and never seen a dagger fashioned quite like this one.

"Mercy daggers were made for ceremonial deaths – putting the target out of their misery as quickly as possible, as the blade is always supposed to be used in such a way that the tip reaches up toward the heart. My mother kept it as her only weapon. Her great grand-mother gave it to her. The Ameroy women have kept it in the family for centuries."

"The Ameroy women?" I questioned. I'd never heard Tejus mention that name before.

"My mother's family name, before she became a Hellswan."

I nodded, even more bowled over by the gift. It was obviously a precious family heirloom, and I felt like I was undeserving of it somehow. I hadn't even known his mother, let alone done anything to warrant receiving something with such sentimental value.

The dagger was beautiful, if not a slightly macabre gift. How very Tejus.

"Here," he proffered the belt that had been attached to him, "you can use this to hold it."

"Put it on?" I asked, moving my robes out of the way –

I was suddenly much less cold.

He leant toward me, wrapping the belt around my waist, moving closer till I could smell his skin—the warm, musky maleness that was so distinct to him. He tightened the buckle and snapped the clasp into place, but instead of moving back again, he paused where he was. My breath started to hitch in my throat and my heart pounded so loudly I thought we could both hear it. I trembled, trying to repress the urge to touch him, as my hunger burnt like a flame inside me.

"Keep your distance," I whispered, stepping back from him.

As I was about to turn away from him, I caught sight of something else.

"Tejus—" I started, not knowing how to convey the sight I saw behind him. I couldn't understand what it was at first—a huge *something* in the sky, like a giant black star-speckled banner. But as I stared, I realized that what I was seeing *was* the sky...only somehow the dawn had been ripped apart to nighttime.

Then the earth started to rumble.

I lurched forward, clutching one of the crenellations for support. The very foundations of the castle were starting to shake, and as I looked wildly over the landscape of Nevertide, I could see a large crack in the earth, running through the forests that surrounded Hellswan and traveling upward toward the Seraq kingdom in the distance. Trees, buildings, the cobbled streets of the village and the small stone houses—everything started tipping toward the crevice jaggedly tearing across the land, sliding downward into its black pit.

"It's started, hasn't it?" I whispered.

This was the work of the entity. I could feel its evil, its malevolent purpose twisting in my gut.

"We need to get out of here," Tejus breathed as the tower started to lurch drunkenly from side to side. The stone walls of the keep started to crumble down to the courtyard, sending plumes of dust exploding upward toward us.

Without waiting for an answer, Tejus picked me up in his arms, cradling me close to his chest.

"Tejus, no!" I cried as I felt myself involuntarily starting to syphon off him.

Ignoring me, he ran down the steps to his living quarters. I begged to be put down again, and then abruptly kept my silence as I saw the devastation of the room—the castle was falling in on us. Half of the floor of Tejus's living quarters had slid down into the floor below. We reached the main staircase just as the tower lurched violently. Tejus ran, panting and pale, down the steps of the tower, the iron creaking and lurching unsteadily.

Run.

The crashing of stone, glass and the fierce explosion of torch fires spreading across the carpets and drapes was deafening. We entered the main hallway and were met with pandemonium.

"We need to get Benedict!" I cried to Tejus, "Julian, Ruby—all of them!" I struggled in his arms as he headed in the opposite direction of the human quarters.

"We're not…going…back," Tejus replied with effort as he picked up the pace, fighting through the hordes of ministers and guards who were creating a mass of bodies, unintentionally blocking the main doorway as they all fought to escape.

"We have to!" I cried, but his grip on me only tightened, rendering my struggles useless. I took one last look behind me as the main arch of the hallway started to collapse in on itself, and then my view was blocked completely by screaming sentries.

Benedict…

ROSE

It's working!

The glow of the stones grew steadily brighter, moving from a faint aura to rays of brilliant color that danced off the faces of the witches, jinn and vamps who surrounded them.

I glanced over at Corrine, who shot me a reassuring smile. The witch, like all the others, was perspiring heavily and looked pale—the magic was obviously taking a lot out of them, but still they continued, determined as I was to get the portal open. Mona was muttering incantations under her breath, her chest heaving as if the words were being ripped from her chest.

Looking down at the black tar, I saw its movements starting to pick up—the heavy sludge-like swirls it had been making since we discovered it now started to splutter and twist. A small opening, no larger than a dime, appeared in the center of the mass. I watched, transfixed, as the opening widened, moving from the circumference of a dime to a fist, and then it was the size of a dinner plate, and I could see the hazy yellow-blue of a morning sky.

A new dimension.

I heard a crackle above the crashing of the waves, and momentarily turned away from the portal, wondering what it was.

"Rose, Rose? Can you hear me?" Caleb's voice blared from the radio—the crackling I'd heard was the transmitter on my breast pocket coming to life. Not wanting to break my connection to Corrine and Claudia, I shoved the on-off button with my chin.

"Caleb!" I cried. "It's working—the portal's opening!"

I heard nothing for a few moments, and then my husband's voice returned.

"I'll tell you why later, but you've got to trust me on this one, Rose—stop opening the portal!"

"What?" I called back, thinking that I'd misheard him. Why would he want us to stop?

"STOP!" he bellowed.

Everyone looked over at me, their concentration broken at the sound of Caleb's voice.

"STOP OPENING THE PORTAL!"

No!

The next world's morning sky started to shrink before my eyes, the tar creeping over the light like a cancer once again.

No…no…no.

Corrine, Mona and the rest of the witches and jinn had released their control of the stones as soon as Caleb's voice emerged from the radio. I watched disbelievingly as my only hope of getting to the children began to shrink before my eyes. I wanted to scream in frustration.

This can't be happening. We were so close!

I looked around at the baffled expressions of the rest of the team. I switched off the radio, needing a few moments before I could listen to the logic and reason behind Caleb's command. Right now, I just didn't care what the danger was – maternal instinct was blindsiding any other thought or feeling. I would have happily faced an apocalypse if it meant I could see my children again…

I watched as Nuriya slowly gathered the stones back into her pouch. The storm had died down almost instantly, leaving an eerie silence to descend on us all, along with a burning question:

What are we going to do now?

I tried to reassure myself that we would find another way… I just couldn't shake the ice-cold fear that time was running out.

READY FOR THE NEXT PART OF THE NOVAK CLAN'S STORY?

Dear Shaddict,

I hope you enjoyed A Power of Old!

The next book, *ASOV 39: A Rip of Realms*, releases January 29th, 2017.

Visit: www.bellaforrest.net for details on purchase.

I'll see you there!

Love,
Bella xxx

P.S. Join my VIP email list and I'll send you a personal reminder as soon as I have a new book out. Visit here to sign up: **www.forrestbooks.com**

(You'll also be the first to receive news about movies/TV show as well as other exciting projects that may be coming up!)

P.P.S. Follow The Shade on Instagram and check out some of the beautiful graphics: @ashadeofvampire

You can also come say hi on Facebook:
www.facebook.com/AShadeOfVampire
And Twitter: @ashadeofvampire

59477782R00195

Made in the USA
Lexington, KY
06 January 2017